History of the First Church in Cmbridge

Anatiposi

Anonymous

History of the First Church in Cmbridge

Reprint of the original, first published in 1872.

1st Edition 2023 | ISBN: 978-3-38212-868-5

Anatiposi Verlag is an imprint of Outlook Verlagsgesellschaft mbH.

Verlag (Publisher): Outlook Verlag GmbH, Zeilweg 44, 60439 Frankfurt, Deutschland
Vertretungsberechtigt (Authorized to represent): E. Roepke, Zeilweg 44, 60439 Frankfurt, Deutschland
Druck (Print): Books on Demand GmbH, In de Tarpen 42, 22848 Norderstedt, Deutschland

HISTORY

OF THE

FIRST CHURCH

IN CAMBRIDGE,

IN CONNECTION WITH THE

SHEPARD CONGREGATIONAL SOCIETY;

WITH ITS

CONFESSION OF FAITH, PRACTICAL RULES, ECCLESIASTICAL PRINCIPLES STANDING RULES, FORM OF ADMISSION, AND THE NAMES OF MEMBERS.

"That thou mayest know how thou oughtest to behave thyself in the house of God, which is the Church of the living God, the pillar and ground of the Truth."

CAMBRIDGE:
PRINTED FOR THE CHURCH AND SOCIETY.
1872.

RIVERSIDE, CAMBRIDGE:
PRINTED BY H. O. HOUGHTON AND COMPANY.

PREFACE.

The following Confession of Faith, Form of Admission, Ecclesiastical Principles, and Rules, were prepared in accordance with a vote of the Church; and after mature, thorough, and prayerful examination were unanimously adopted, and, together with some historical notices, ordered to be printed for the use of the members. The work is now presented to the Church with the earnest prayer, that, through the influence of Divine grace, it may be instrumental in bringing us all in "the unity of the faith, and of the knowledge of the Son of God, unto a perfect man, unto the measure of the stature of the fulness of Christ: that we henceforth be no more children, tossed to and fro, and carried about with every wind of doctrine, by the sleight of men, and cunning craftiness, whereby they lie in wait to deceive: but speaking the truth in love, may grow up into him in all things, which is the head, even Christ: from whom the whole body fitly joined together and compacted by that which every joint supplieth, according to the effectual working in the measure of every part, maketh increase of the body unto the edifying of itself in love."

Cambridge, 1872.

PASSAGES

IN THE

HISTORY OF THE FIRST CHURCH

IN CAMBRIDGE.

"I know thy works, and charity, and service, and faith, and thy patience, and thy works; and the last to be more than the first."

EXTRACT

FROM THE PREFACE TO THE CONFESSION OF FAITH ADOPTED BY THE CHURCHES OF MASSACHUSETTS IN 1680.

What hours of temptation may overtake these churches, is not for us to say. Only the Lord doth many times so order things, that when his people have made a good confession, they shall be put upon the trial one way or other, to see whether they have (or who among them hath not) been sincere in what they have done. The Lord grant that the loins of our minds may be so girt about with truth, that we may be able to withstand in the evil day, and having done all, to stand.

PASSAGES

IN THE

HISTORY OF THE FIRST CHURCH

IN CAMBRIDGE.

The settlement of Cambridge, originally called Newtown, was commenced in the spring of the year 1631. The town was considerably enlarged by the arrival of a number of emigrants, called the "Braintree Company," in August, 1632. As the quiet enjoyment of religious privileges was the great object of their removal to this place, their first work was to erect a house for public worship, and adopt measures for the establishment of the ministry and the ordinances of the gospel among them. It was a common remark of the early settlers of New England, that a country destitute of the gospel ministry resembled paradise without the tree of life.

Many of the emigrants had, while in England, belonged to the congregation of the Rev. Thomas Hooker, a preacher of great celebrity, who, to escape fines and imprisonment for non-conformity, had fled into Holland. Being greatly attached to him, and wishing to enjoy again the benefits of his able ministry, they invited him to come and take the pastoral charge of them. In compliance with their earnest entreaty, Mr. Hooker left Holland, and having persuaded Mr. Samuel Stone, a man of like spirit, to accompany him as an assistant in the ministry, took passage for New England, and arrived at Boston September 4, 1633. Mr. Hooker was immediately chosen Pastor, and Mr. Stone Teacher, of the people of Newtown; and on the 11th of October, after solemn fasting and prayer, they were ordained to their respective offices. Early in the summer of 1636, the whole church and congregation, consisting of about a hundred persons, removed to Connecticut, and commenced the settlement of Hartford.

In October, 1635, the Rev. Thomas Shepard arrived at Boston, from England, with the people who were to constitute his society. Having purchased the houses and lands which Mr. Hooker's congregation were about to leave, they made arrangements for establishing themselves at Newtown, until they should find a more suitable place. "But after having been here some time," says Mr. Shepard, in his autobiography, "divers of our brethren did desire to sit still and not to remove farther; partly because of the fellowship of the churches, partly because they thought their lives were short and removals to near plantations full of troubles, partly because they found sufficient for themselves and their company. Hereupon there was a purpose to enter into church fellowship"; and on the first day of February, 1636, a public assembly was convened, and a church, the first permanent one in Cambridge, and the eleventh in the Colony of Massachusetts, was solemnly organized. The following account of this transaction is taken from "Winthrop's Journal": —

"Mr. Shepard a godly minister, come lately out of England, and divers other good christians, intending to raise a church body, came and acquainted the magistrates therewith, who gave their approbation. They also sent to all the neighbouring churches for their elders to give their assistance at a certain day at Newtown, when they should constitute their body. Accordingly at this day there met a great assembly, where the proceeding was as followeth.

"Mr. Shepard and two others who were after to be chosen to office, sat together in the elders' seat; then the elder of them began with prayer, after this Mr. Shepard prayed with deep confession of sin, &c. and exercised out of Eph. v. that he might make it to himself a holy, &c. and also opened the cause of their meeting. Then the elder desired to know of the churches assembled what number were needful to make a church, and how they ought to proceed in this action. Whereupon some of the ancient ministers conferring shortly together gave answer,—That the scripture did not set down any certain rule for the number, three (they thought) were too few, because by Matt. xviii. an appeal was allowed from three, but that seven might be a fit number; and for their proceeding they advised, that such as were to join should make confession of their faith, and declare what work of grace the Lord had wrought in them, which accordingly they did, Mr. Shepard first, then four others, then the elder and one who was to be deacon (who had also prayed) and another member; then the covenant was read, and they all gave a solemn assent to it. Then the elder desired of the churches, that if they did approve them to be a church, they would give them the right hand of fellowship. Whereupon Mr. Cotton (upon short speech with some other near him) in the name of the churches, gave his hand to the elder, with a short speech of their assent, and desired the peace of the Lord's presence to be with them. Then Mr. Shepard made an exhortation to the rest of his body about the nature of their covenant, and to stand firm to it, and commended them to the Lord in a most heavenly prayer. Then the elder told the assembly that they were intended to choose Mr. Shepard for their pastor (by the name of the brother who had exercised) and desired the churches that if they had anything to except against him, they would impart it to them before the day of ordination. Then he gave the churches thanks for their assistance, and so left them to the Lord."

Mr. Shepard's ordination took place soon after, though the precise date of it is not known. "It was deferred," says Mather, "until another day, wherein there was more time to go through the other solemnities proper to such an occasion."

Mr. Shepard died of a quinsy August 25, 1649, in the forty-fourth year of his age, after a most able and successful ministry of thirteen years. He was one of the most eminent of the early divines of New England. His preaching was in demonstration of the spirit and with power. It is said that he seldom delivered a discourse that did not produce a decided and saving impression upon his people. His practical writings are still of great value. He was as much distinguished for his piety, industry, and vigilance as a pastor, as for his talents and learning. Such was the public opinion of him, and of his ministry, that "when the foundation of a college was to be laid in this State, Cambridge, rather than any other place, was chosen to be the seat of that happy seminary; out of which there proceeded many notable preachers, who were made such, very much by their sitting under Mr. Shepard's enlightening and powerful ministry."[1]

The doctrinal basis of the church at its organization has never been changed, and is set forth in the "Confession of Faith" which follows this sketch of its history.

The following is a list of the ministers of the First Church in Cambridge from its organization, in 1636, until the settlement of Dr. Holmes, in 1792:—

THOMAS SHEPARD, ordained February 1636; died August 25, 1649, aged 44.

JONATHAN MITCHEL, ordained August 21, 1650; died July 9, 1668, aged 43.

URIAN OAKES, ordained November 8, 1671; died July 25, 1681, aged 50.

NATHANIEL GOOKIN, ordained November 15, 1682; died August 7, 1692, aged 34.

[1] Mather's *Magnalia*, Book III. Chapter 5. Those who wish to obtain more knowledge of the first Pastor of this Church, are referred to to the *Biography of Thomas Shepard*, by Rev. J. A. ALBRO, D. D.

WILLIAM BRATTLE, ordained November 25, 1696; died February 15, 1717, aged 55.

NATHANIEL APPLETON, ordained October 9, 1717; died February 9, 1784, aged 91.

TIMOTHY HILLIARD, installed October 27, 1783; died May 9, 1790, aged 44.[1]

On the 19th of October, 1791, the church elected the Rev. ABIEL HOLMES their pastor, as the successor of Mr. Hilliard; and the parish, upon receiving official notice of his election, voted concurrence. A council was accordingly convened, and Dr. Holmes was solemnly installed Pastor of the First Church and Society in Cambridge, on the 25th of January, 1792.

During a period of thirty-five years Dr. Holmes enjoyed the confidence and affection of the people of his pastoral charge, and his labors among them were not without good fruit. Entire harmony also existed between the church and society. In 1827 difficulties arose; which, after a protracted and painful controversy, terminated in the separation of the church from the parish, and the organization of a new ecclesiastical society, with which the church is still in connection. The following account of those proceedings is transcribed from the records of the church.

"The first notice of dissatisfaction with the ministry, or of disaffection to the person of the pastor, was expressed in a memorial signed by a number of the parishioners, dated July 9, 1827, and presented to the pastor on the 20th of the same month. The ground of the memorial was the discontinuance of pastoral exchanges with ministers with whom

[1] For biographical notices of these learned, able, and pious ministers, see Rev. Dr. HOLMES'S *History of Cambridge*, and Rev. Dr. SPRAGUE'S *Annals of the American Pulpit*, also the *Lectures upon the History of the First Church in Cambridge*, by the present pastor.

he had formerly exchanged services. A discontinuance of pulpit exchanges between ministers of different religious principles had begun long before, by mutual and tacit consent. The more open avowal of Unitarianism at this, than at any former period, very sensibly affected ministerial intercourse, and many ministers, who had formerly exchanged services, now discontinued them without controversy and without blame.

"To the memorial of the parishioners the pastor gave a written answer, in which he asked their indulgence in candidly presenting to them the difficulties and dangers that might be apprehended from so diversified and indefinite a course of public service as their memorial appeared to have for its object; and expressed his persuasion, that they would consider his reply with the same candor with which he endeavored to consider their memorial, and that they would allow their minister the same liberty of conscience which he allowed to them."

A correspondence between a committee of the memorialists and the pastor succeeded. Parish meetings were at length held, against whose measures remonstrances and memorials were presented by a number of the parishioners and by the church; and in December, 1828, the parish, deeming it unnecessary to take any further order in relation to the memorials and papers, proposed the calling of a mutual ecclesiastical council.

The church, by a committee chosen to express to the pastor their views and feelings in relation to the recent measures adopted by the parish, presented to him an address on the 9th of January, 1829. After a review of the proceedings of the parish, the church say: "These facts, with many other considerations that might be urged, serve to show, that a radical change in your ministrations, if not in your opinions, was what could alone satisfy the memorialists. Under these circumstances, the church has manifested a willingness, and has voted to coöperate with the parish in calling a mutual council. This offer was rejected, under circumstances not altogether favorable to a reconciliation of existing difficulties, and, as we believe, without a due regard to the rights of the church, as a party deeply concerned in the result."

The address was closed with these words: "From a careful and impartial view, therefore, of the whole subject, the undersigned, in behalf of the church, feel constrained to believe, that a sense of duty, a regard to the honor, the interest, and the permanent good of the people under your pastoral care, have been the governing motives which have influenced you in the decisions made upon the several propositions submitted by the parish."

The pastor made a communication to the committee of the parish on the 29th of January, on the subject of a mutual council; in which he declared his ready consent to their proposal, if the council were regularly called, according to the usage of our churches, and to the express desire of this church, and other respectable parishioners. But neither the parish, nor its committee, would allow the church any participation in the affair, nor admit its claims to a concurrent voice with the pastor.

An ex parte council, called by the committee authorized by a former vote of the parish, convened on the 19th of May, 1829, and recommended to the parish to terminate the contract subsisting between them and their minister. On the 8th of June, the parish voted to accept the result of that council, and declared the pastor's connection with the parish to be dissolved. The pastor, on receiving a copy of these transactions from the parish clerk, replied by referring to his protest against the jurisdiction of the ex parte council, and added, that he still considered himself as the lawful minister of the parish, and held himself ready to perform any and all of the duties, in or out of the pulpit, which belonged to his office as pastor of the First Church and Society in Cambridge.

The church, with other parishioners who had protested against the proceedings of the parish, and against the jurisdiction of the ex parte council, together with other aggrieved members of the society, considering Dr. Holmes as still their pastor, and knowing that he was ready to perform any duties pertaining to his pastoral office, were disposed to meet together with one accord, in one place, for an appropriate observance of the Lord's day. Their disposition and desire being made known to their pastor, with information that they would assemble at the Old Court House on the ensuing Sabbath, at the usual hour of divine service, their pastor met them there, and performed the service to a full, attentive, and solemn assembly.

An advisory council, being called by letters missive from the pastor and the church, convened at Cambridge on the 17th of June. The result shows, that this council are "unanimously of the opinion that Dr. Holmes has not, in any way, forfeited his office as Pastor of the First Church and Parish in Cambridge; and that he is still, according to ecclesiastical usage, the pastor and minister of said church and parish"; and that they "approve the course pursued by him in continuing to perform parochial duties wherever and to whomsoever he may have opportunity; and advise him and the church, and other friends of truth, not to forsake the assembling of themselves together, but to maintain divine worship and the celebration of divine ordinances."

The church, at a notified meeting held June 25th, voted unanimously: "That the result of the council, called by the church and its pastor on the 17th instant, meets its approbation; and that the counsel and advice therein contained will be, by divine aid, religiously followed." Divine service was accordingly held, statedly, by the pastor and church, with a respectable number of the society, at the Court House, until a house of worship was erected for their use. The whole number of members belonging to the church at that time was about ninety, full two thirds of whom followed the pastor and attended on his ministry. The number of male members was twenty-one, fifteen of whom were the uniform friends and supporters of the pastor, and two, only, took an active part in the measures of the parish.

A society, composed of persons who adhered to the church and its pastor, had been recently organized for the purpose of supporting the gospel here as it had been held and taught since the formation of the church, by the name of "The Shepard Congregational Society." With this society the church, as a body, was, on the 12th of November, respectfully invited to unite and coöperate, according to the rights and usages of Congregational churches.

The pastor, not being legally dismissed from office in the First Parish, could not consistently attach himself to the new society, and become, in form, its minister. In consideration of these circumstances, the church, having consulted with their pastor, "whose relation to us," they said, "we wish to hold sacred and inviolable," and "finding that, in present circumstances, the choice of a colleague-pastor meets with his entire approbation," voted: "That until such time as our rights, with those of our pastor, shall be respected, and the privileges of the gospel ministry be enjoyed, as heretofore, in connection with the First Parish in Cambridge, we will, as a church, accede to the invitation of the said Shepard Congregational Society, and coöperate with it in maintaining the worship and ordinances of the gospel, according to the established principles and usages of Congregational churches in this Commonwealth."

In pursuance of the object, and subject to the conditions of the preceding vote, the church proceeded to invite and call Mr. NEHEMIAH ADAMS, Jr., to the office of colleague-pastor in this church, in connection with the Rev. Dr. Holmes as senior pastor.

A committee was then chosen, to communicate a copy of the preamble and votes to the Shepard Society, and request their concurrence; and in case of their concurrence, to communicate to Mr. Adams the doings of the church, and in case of his acceptance of the call, to take all due and usual measures in relation to his ordination. Mr. Adams accepted the call, and was accordingly ordained as colleague-pastor of the First Church in Cambridge, on the 17th day of December, 1829.

A lot of land having been given by Miss Sarah Ann Dana, and funds sufficient to defray the expense of erecting a suitable house for public worship having been obtained, the ground was broken for that purpose on the 5th day of August, 1830. At six o'clock in the morning of that day, the members of the church, with their pastors, repaired to the spot, where a prayer was offered by the junior pastor, and a hymn was sung; after which the senior pastor briefly stated the causes which had brought them to that place, offered a prayer, and, after the singing of another hymn, pronounced a benediction.

The corner-stone of the house of worship for the First Church, in connection with the Shepard Congregational Society in Cambridge, was laid, with appropriate ceremonies, September 21, 1830. The solemnity was introduced with an address by the senior pastor; an ode, adapted to the occasion, was then sung; then a prayer was offered by the senior pastor; a pastoral letter was read from the junior pastor, absent on account of sickness, was read; an address and prayer by the Rev. Samuel Green, of Boston, followed; and the exercises were concluded by a benediction.

On this occasion, a silver plate, inclosed in a leaden box presented by a Christian friend, was placed under the corner-stone, with this inscription: —

TO

JESUS CHRIST

AND

THE CHURCH,

THE PILLAR AND GROUND OF THE TRUTH.

FIRST CHURCH AND SHEPARD SOCIETY,

IN CAMBRIDGE:

ABIEL HOLMES,
NEHEMIAH ADAMS, } *Pastors;*

WILLIAM HILLIARD,
JAMES MUNROE, } *Deacons;*

XXI SEPTEMBER, MDCCCXXX.

The Corner-stone was laid after the introductory address by the senior pastor; and, while laying the stone, he pronounced the following words: —

The Church is built upon the Apostles and Prophets, JESUS CHRIST himself being the chief Corner-stone. Other foundation can no man lay than that is laid, which is Jesus Christ. May the stone which we now lay be a true emblem of the great Corner-stone upon which the First Church in Cambridge was originally built, and a pledge of its permanent continuance upon the same everlasting foundation, JESUS CHRIST, the same yesterday, to-day, and forever.

b

The house of worship, the corner-stone of which had been thus laid, was dedicated to God the Father, Son, and Holy Ghost, on the 23d of February, 1831. The exercises at the Dedication were: An Introductory Anthem; Reading of the Scriptures; Consecration Anthem; Prayer; Hymn; Sermon by the Senior pastor, from Jeremiah vi. 18; Prayer; Original Hymn by the Junior pastor; Benediction.

In the month of August, 1831, the Deacon of the Church of the First Parish in Cambridge, commenced a suit at law against William Hilliard and James Munroe, in their capacity as Deacons of the First Church in Cambridge, to recover certain articles of church property, as set forth in the writ, and held them to answer to a plea of the case, in the penal sum of five thousand dollars. As it had been ascertained that, in a case believed to be similar to this, the Supreme Judicial Court of this Commonwealth had decided that church property, so-called, belongs to the parish, or to such members of the church as shall adhere to the parish in case of a separation, the church, at a regular meeting, appointed a committee, who were "authorized and empowered, with legal advice thereto, further to defend according to the circumstances that might be found to exist, or to deliver up to the demandant all such property of the church, as should be specified in the schedule annexed to the writ, in the suit of said demandant, and to take his legal discharge therefor."

The committee appointed under this vote, having obtained legal advice upon the subject referred to them, delivered up the church property to the plaintiff, and on the 28th day of December the following instrument was executed by him: —

"Know all men by these presents, that I, Abel Whitney, Deacon of the First Church in Cambridge, in behalf of said church, have this day received of Deacon William Hilliard and Deacon James Munroe, the property constituting the church fund and poor's fund, belonging to said church, amounting, in money and securities for money, to the sum of four thousand one hundred and fifty-four dollars and three cents; also, the communion-service of said church, consisting of four silver tankards, seven silver cups, one silver spoon, six britannia dishes, two napkins, one table cloth and basin, four books of church records, and sundry files of papers, and a trunk and box containing the same; also, the library of books, with the shelves for the same, and nine dollars and ninety-nine cents for the same."

The decision of the Supreme Court in accordance with which this property was surrendered, determined only the *civil rights* of the Church, and did not affect its *ecclesiastical* position, by virtue of which it remains "The First Church in Cambridge."

The church fund, for the recovery of which this suit was brought, was originally constituted by the donation of fifty pounds, by a member of the church, and increased to the above-mentioned sum entirely by contributions of the church members at the Lord's Supper. A part of the church plate, above referred to, was given to the church, and the rest was purchased with its own funds.

It may be interesting to state, in this connection, that, while the church was suffering great inconvenience from the loss of its table furniture, the manuscript "Autobiography of THOMAS SHEPARD" was providentially obtained by Mr. Adams, and a sufficient number of copies were printed to defray the expense of a suitable communion-service, which is still in use. Thus, after a period of nearly two hundred years, the founder of the church was permitted to furnish it with the means of celebrating the ordinances of the gospel.

In September, 1831, the senior pastor, laboring under continued and increasing debility, unable to perform stated, and seldom able to perform occasional service, asked the consent of the church to his retiring from the pastoral cares. The church consented to the request, and united with the pastor in calling a council, to sanction the procedure, if it should see fit. The council convened on the 26th of September, 1831, and after due deliberation, sanctioned the proposed dissolution of the pastoral connection between Dr. Holmes and the church. Their decision is thus declared in their Result: —

"A Letter from the senior pastor of the First Church in Cambridge, requesting a dissolution of the pastoral connection that has subsisted between them for nearly forty years, on account of advanced age and infirmity, together with the reply of the church, consenting to such a dissolution, and uniting in the choice of a council for carrying it into effect, if they see proper, were laid before the council. Whereupon voted: That, in the opinion of this Council, the reasons assigned by the senior pastor for the dissolution of his pastoral relation, and the consent on the part of the church, are satisfactory; and that the pastoral relation between the Rev. Dr. Holmes and the First Church in Cambridge, be, and accordingly it is, hereby dissolved.

"It is with mingled emotions of pain and satisfaction, that this Council have attended to the business for which they have been convened. While they deeply regret the occasion that has led to their result, in the bodily infirmities attending the advancing age of the venerated and beloved senior pastor of the First Church in Cambridge, they are most happy in the reflection that the ministerial and Christian character of Dr. Holmes is unspotted; that he has been enabled, by divine grace, to bear the peculiar trials to which he has been called in the course of his ministry, with exemplary wisdom, firmness, meekness, and patience; and that, in the circumstances attending the dissolution of his pastoral connection, a spirit of union and harmony has been manifested by the respective parties so deeply interested.

"It is unnecessary for this Council to add anything by way of testimonial and recommendation to a character so well known in this Commonwealth, in this country, and in Europe, as that of the late pastor of the First Church in Cambridge; the long tried and highly esteemed friend of learning and religion. His works are his testimonial, and his praise is in all the churches."

Dr. Holmes preached his Farewell sermon on the 2d of October, 1831. He died in the exercise of strong faith, and in the comforts of a hope full of immortality, on the 12th day of June, 1837, in the seventy-fourth year of his age.

Within three years after the dismission of Dr. Holmes, the church was called upon to part with its remaining pastor. On the 22d of February, 1834, the Rev. Mr. Adams having received an invitation from the Essex Street Church and Society, in Boston, to become their pastor, and believing it to be his duty to accept it, requested the church and society to unite with him in calling an ecclesiastical council to dissolve his ministerial connection with them. This request was complied with, though with great reluctance, and a council was accordingly invited to assemble at Cambridge for this purpose. The council met on the 14th of March following; and after serious deliberation, unanimously dismissed Mr. Adams, with a view to his acceptance of the call from Boston.

On the 30th of January, 1835, the church unanimously elected the Rev. John Adams Albro their pastor, and the society concurred in the choice. Mr. Albro signified his acceptance of their call by letter, dated March 28th; and on the 15th of April following, he was regularly installed pastor of the church and society by an ecclesiastical council duly called for that purpose.

After a ministry in this church of thirty years, Dr. Albro, at his own urgent desire, was dismissed from this pastorate on the 15th of April, 1865. He continued to reside in the parsonage until December, 1866, when he died at the age of sixty-seven years, after a brief illness, in West Roxbury, where his last public service was performed. His ministry was full of usefulness, and under his care this church and society largely increased. He died amid the lamentations of the people he had served so long, and was buried from the sanctuary where he had ministered unto them in holy things. He left abounding works to praise him. His name and fame are abroad among the churches. His memory is fragrant and blessed.

In 1865, the Rev. ALEXANDER McKENZIE was invited to the pastoral care of the church and society. For imperative reasons the invitation was declined; but upon its renewal, in the following year, it was accepted; and he was installed on the 24th of January, 1867.

It is impossible now to ascertain the names and characters of all those who have held the office of Elder and of Deacon in this church, from its organization; but a list, as complete as it could be made, will be found in the Catalogue at the end of this book. At the time of its separation from the First Parish, and union with the Shepard Congregational Society, which may be regarded as an important epoch in its history, William Hilliard and James Munroe were its Deacons. Deacon Hilliard died April 27, 1836. Deacon Munroe died in 1848. Of each of these church officers it could be said, he was an honest and good man, "not double-tongued, not greedy of filthy lucre, holding the mystery of the faith in a pure conscience." They "used the office of deacon well, and purchased to themselves a good degree, and great boldness in the faith which is in Christ Jesus."

On the 21st of April, 1837, Mr. Stephen T. Farwell was chosen Deacon, in the place of Mr. Hilliard; and on the 30th of the same month, he was solemnly set apart to the office by prayer, according to the ancient usage of the Congregational churches. Deacon Charles W. Homer was chosen to this office in 1848, and was duly installed on the 4th of January, 1849.

The number of Deacons was subsequently increased to four; and, on the 2d of July, 1869, Mr. Charles Theodore Russell and Mr. George S. Saunders were solemnly set apart for the duties of the office. Mr. Russell retired from the office in 1871.

This church has occupied five houses of worship, and the sixth is nearly ready for dedication as this sketch closes.

We conclude this brief history of our ancient church in the words of Solomon: "Blessed be the Lord, that hath given rest unto his people, according to all that he promised; there hath not failed one word of all his good promise, which he promised by the hand of Moses his servant. The Lord our God be with us, as he was with our fathers; let him not leave us, nor forsake us; that he may incline our hearts unto him, to walk in all his ways, and to keep his commandments, and his statutes, and his judgments, which he commanded our fathers. And let the words wherewith we have made supplication before the Lord, be nigh unto the Lord day and night, that he maintain the cause of his people at all times, as the matter shall require; that all the people of the earth may know that the Lord is God, and that there is none else."

CONFESSION OF FAITH.

That ye may with one mind and one mouth glorify God, even the Father of our Lord Jesus Christ.

For with the heart man believeth unto righteousness; and with the mouth confession is made unto salvation.

This CONFESSION is in substance, and for the most part in language, taken from the "Confession of Faith owned and consented unto by the Elders and Messengers of the Churches assembled at Boston, May 12, 1680;" which is the basis of the Confessions of all the Orthodox Congregational Churches in New England. It expresses the views of this Church upon matters of doctrine through its entire history.

CONFESSION OF FAITH.

OF THE BEING OF GOD.

THERE is one only living and true GOD,[1] who is alone in and unto himself all-sufficient,[2] the fountain of life and being, of whom and through whom are all things visible and invisible,[3] to whom all intelligent creatures are bound to render supreme homage, love, and obedience.[4]

[1] Deut. vi. 4. [2] Acts xvii. 24, 25. [3] Col. i. 16, 17. [4] Rev. v. 11-14.

OF THE HOLY SCRIPTURES.

ALTHOUGH the light of nature, and the works of creation and providence, do so far reveal the being and attributes of God, as to leave men inexcusable in their unbelief,[1] yet it has pleased him to reveal himself, and to declare his will more fully and clearly, in the Scriptures of the Old and New Testaments,[2] which were written by divine inspiration,[3] and are given to mankind by God's authority,[4] as a sufficient revelation of all things necessary to salvation,[5] and the only perfect and infallible rule of faith and practice,[6] by which all doctrines and commandments of men are to be tried, and all religious controversies are to be determined.[7]

[1] Rom. i. 19, 20. [2] Heb. i. 1, 2; Gal. i. 11, 12. [3] 2 Peter i. 21. [4] 1 Thess. ii. 13. [5] 2 Tim. iii. 16, 17. [6] Rev. xxii. 18, 19; Gal. i. 8. [7] Isaiah viii. 20.

OF THE DIVINE ATTRIBUTES.

God is a most pure and perfect spirit,[1] self-existent,[2] eternal,[3] immutable,[4] infinite and incomprehensible[5] in holiness,[6] wisdom,[7] benevolence,[8] and power;[9] the rewarder of them that diligently seek him;[10] long-suffering, abundant in goodness and truth;[11] ready to forgive, and plenteous in mercy to all that call upon him;[12] most just and righteous in all his counsels, works, commands, and judgments.[13]

[1] John iv. 24.
[2] John v. 26.
[3] Psalm xc. 2.
[4] James i. 17.
[5] Job xi. 7–9.
[6] Isaiah vi. 3.
[7] Rom. xi. 33.
[8] 1 John iv. 8.
[9] Gen. xvii. 1.
[10] Heb. xi. 6.
[11] Exod. xxxiv. 6, 7.
[12] Psalm lxxxvi. 5.
[13] Psalm xxxiii. 4; Rom. vii. 12; Rev. xvi. 7.

OF THE TRINITY.

In the unity of the Godhead there are three persons of one substance, power, and eternity; the Father, Son, and Holy Ghost.[1]

[1] Matt. xxviii. 19; John i. 1–3, 14; xv. 26; 2 Cor. xiii. 14.

OF DIVINE PROVIDENCE.

God upholds,[1] directs, disposes, and governs all creatures and things, from the greatest to the least,[2] by his most wise and holy providence,[3] according to his infallible foreknowledge,[4] and the free and immutable counsel of his own will,[5] to the glory of his wisdom, power, justice, goodness, and mercy.[6]

[1] Hebrews i. 3. [2] Psalm cxxxv. 6; Matt. x. 29–31. [3] Prov. xv. 3; 2 Chron. xvi. 9. [4] Acts xv. 18. [5] Eph. i. 11. [6] Eph. iii. 10; Psalm cxlv. 7.

OF THE CREATION AND FALL OF MAN.

God created the first parents of our race with rational and immortal souls,[1] endued with knowledge, righteousness, and true holiness, after his own image,[2] and gave them a holy law with the promise of life to them, and in them to their posterity, upon condition of perfect and personal obedience;[3] but they voluntarily transgressing the divine command, in eating the forbidden fruit,[4] fell from their state of original righteousness and communion with God,[5] into a state of sin and death;[6] in consequence of which, they being the root, and the public representatives of all mankind,[7] their whole posterity are by nature alienated from God,[8] entirely unholy and corrupt,[9] inclined to all evil,[10] under the condemnation of the divine law,[11] and subject to death, temporal and eternal.[12]

1 Gen. ii. 7; Matt. x. 28.
2 Gen. i. 26.
3 Gen. ii. 16, 17; Rom. ii. 14, 15; x. 5.
4 Rom. ii. 15; Gen. iii. 6.
5 Gen. iii. 7, 8; Rom. iii. 23.
6 Gen. iii. 17-19.
7 Acts xvii. 26.
8 Rom. viii. 7; Eph. iv. 18.
9 Gen. vi. 5; Psalm li. 1; Jer. xvii. 9.
10 Rom. iii. 10-12; vii. 19.
11 Gal. iii. 10; John iii. 18; Eph. ii. 3.
12 James i. 14, 15; 1 Cor. xv. 21, 22; Rom. vi. 23; Matt. xxv. 41.

OF THE REDEEMER.

The Son of God, the second person in the Trinity, in accordance with an eternal purpose of grace,[1] freely undertook the work of redeeming and saving fallen men;[2] and when the fullness of time was come,[3] he took upon him man's nature,[4] with all its essential properties and common infirmities,[5] yet without sin,[6] being born of the Virgin Mary, by the power of the Holy Ghost;[7] was

1 Eph. iii. 9-12. 2 1 Tim. ii. 6. 3 Gal. iv. 4. 4 John i. 1, 14; Phil. ii. 7, 8.
5 Heb. ii. 17. 6 Heb. vii. 26; 1 Pet. ii. 22. 7 Luke i. 27, 31, 35.

made under, and perfectly fulfilled, the divine Law given to men;[1] suffered in soul and in body for our sins,[2] the just for the unjust,[3] and became obedient unto death, even the death of the cross;[4] and having, by his perfect obedience,[5] sufferings,[6] and sacrifice of himself,[7] which he through the eternal Spirit once offered up to God,[8] made a full and complete atonement for sin,[9] and obtained eternal redemption for all that obey him,[10] he rose from the dead,[11] and ascended into heaven to the glory which he had with the Father before the world was,[12] where he ever liveth to make intercession for us,[13] and from whence he will come to judge both the living and the dead at the end of the world.[14]

1 Gal. iv. 4; Matt. v. 17.
2 Matthew xxvi. 37, 38; xxvii. 46.
3 1 Peter iii. 18.
4 Phil. ii. 8.
5 Rom. v. 19.
6 Heb. ii. 10.
7 Heb. ix. 26.
8 Heb. ix. 14.
9 Rom. iii. 25, 26; v. 11.
10 Heb. v. 9.
11 1 Cor. xv. 4.
12 Luke xxiv. 50, 51; John xvii. 5.
13 Rom. viii. 34; Heb. vii. 25.
14 Acts i. 11; Rom. xiv. 9, 10; Matt. xxv. 31-46.

OF THE HOLY GHOST.

THE Holy Ghost, proceeding from the Father and the Son,[1] is the only author of regeneration,[2] sanctification,[3] and new spiritual life and obedience in man;[4] and without his gracious and effectual work in the soul, no sinner can ever enter into the kingdom of God.[5]

1 John xiv. 26. 2 John i. 12, 13; iii. 5. 3 Rom. xv. 16; 2 Thess. ii. 13.
4 Rom. viii. 2; 1 Peter i. 2. 5 Ezek. xxxvi. 26, 27; John vi. 37, 44; iii. 5, 6.

OF ELECTION.

GOD, from eternity, according to his immutable purpose, and the most wise and holy counsel of his own will,[1] hath chosen in Christ a great number of the fallen race of Adam unto everlasting life and glory,[2] to the praise of his free and sovereign grace.[3]

1 Eph. i. 4, 11; 2 Tim. i. 9. 2 Eph. i. 5, 11; 2 Thess. ii. 13; John xv. 19; Rom. vi. 23. 3 Eph. i. 6, 12; Phil. i. 11; 1 Peter ii. 9, 10.

OF EFFECTUAL CALLING, JUSTIFICATION, ADOPTION, SANCTIFICATION, PERSEVERANCE.

All those whom God hath chosen unto eternal life, he *effectually calls*,[1] by his Word and Spirit,[2] out of that state of sin and death in which they are by nature, to a state of grace and salvation by Jesus Christ;[3] enlightening their minds spiritually and savingly to understand divine things,[4] inclining them to that which is good,[5] and effectually drawing them to Christ,[6] yet so, that they come most freely, being made willing by his grace.[7]

1 Matt. ix. 13; Rom. viii. 28, 30. 2 2 Thess. ii. 13, 14. 3 2 Tim. i. 9, 10; Eph. ii. 1-8. 4 Acts xxvi. 18. 5 Phil. ii. 13; Ezek. xi. 19, 20. 6 John vi. 37-45. 7 Psalm cx. 3.

He *justifies* them freely,[1] by pardoning their sins,[2] and accepting them as righteous;[3] not on account of any works of righteousness done by them,[4] but solely for Christ's sake, through faith in his blood.[5]

1 Rom. iii. 24. 2 2 Cor. v. 19, 21; Heb. viii. 12. 3 Rom. v. 19. 4 Titus iii. 5, 7; Rom. iv. 6. 5 Rom. iii. 20-26; Eph. ii. 8.

He grants unto them the grace of *adoption*,[1] by which they are taken into the number, and enjoy the privileges of God's children,[2] receive the spirit of adoption whereby they are enabled to cry, Abba, Father; the Spirit itself bearing witness that they are the children of God,[3] are

1 Eph. i. 5. 2 Rom. viii. 17. 3 Rom. viii. 15, 16.

sealed to the day of redemption,[1] and inherit the promises as heirs of salvation.[2]

1 Eph. iv. 30. 2 Heb. vi. 12; 1 Peter i. 4.

He *sanctifies* them by his Word and Spirit, dwelling in them;[1] destroying the dominion of sin,[2] creating a clean heart, and renewing a right spirit within them,[3] working in them all that which is well pleasing in his sight,[4] and strengthening them to the practice of true holiness, without which no man shall see the Lord.[5]

1 Eph. v. 26; 2 Thess. ii. 13. 2 Rom. vi. 6–14. 3 Col. iii. 10; Psalm li. 10. 4 Heb. xiii. 21. 5 Col. i. 11; Heb. xii. 14.

Finally, though they often grieve his Holy Spirit by their sins,[1] he does not permit them to fall totally and finally from the state of grace; but keeps them by his power, through faith, unto eternal salvation.[2]

1 Eph. iv. 30; Isaiah lxiv. 7, 9. 2 Phil. i. 6; John x. 28, 29; xvii. 11–24; 1 Peter, i. 3–7.

OF GOOD WORKS.

Although we cannot merit pardon of sin, or eternal life by any works of our own,[1] it is our duty to live a godly, righteous, and sober life, according to the will of God;[2] and by good works, done in obedience to the divine law,[3] and by the grace of Christ working in us,[4] we are to show the genuineness of our faith,[5] manifest our thankfulness,[6] strengthen our assurance,[7] adorn our profession of the gospel,[8] and glorify God,[9] whose work-

1 Rom. iii. 20; Eph. ii. 8, 9. 2 Titus ii. 12; Rom. xii. 1, 2. 3 Micah vi. 8; Rom. vii. 12. 4 John xv. 5, 6. 5 James ii. 18, 22. 6 1 Peter ii. 9. 7 John ii. 3, 5; 2 Peter i. 5–10. 8 Titus ii. 5–10. 9 Matt. v. 16; John xv. 8.

manship we are, created in Christ Jesus thereunto,[1] that, having our fruit unto holiness, we may have the end eternal life.[2]

1 Eph. ii. 10. 2 Rom. vi. 22.

OF REPENTANCE AND FAITH.

In the gospel, pardon and eternal life are freely offered to sinners, upon condition of repentance towards God,[1] and faith in the Lord Jesus Christ;[2] and without these evangelical graces no man can be saved.[3]

1 Isaiah lv. 7; Luke xxiv. 47. 2 Acts xvi. 31; John i. 12. 3 Acts xvii. 30; John iii. 36.

OF THE MINISTRY OF THE WORD.

The ministry of the word being the divinely appointed means whereby, ordinarily, sinners are turned from darkness to light, and from the power of Satan unto God,[1] all persons are required and encouraged to attend upon this ordinance,[2] with dependence upon the influence of the Holy Ghost, without which no means are sufficient for their conversion;[3] and all hope of salvation in voluntary neglect of it is presumptuous and vain.[4]

1 Luke xxiv. 47; Rom. x. 14–17. 2 Isaiah lv. 3; Acts x. 22; xiii. 7, 44. 3 John xiv. 26; Acts i. 2, 8; 1 Thess. i. 5, 6. 4 Heb. x. 25; xii. 25.

OF THE CHURCH.

God has a visible church upon earth;[1] which is represented in the Scriptures as a holy, spiritual kingdom,[2]

1 1 Tim. iii. 15; Acts xx. 28. 2 1 Peter ii. 9; Eph. v. 26, 27.

established upon the foundation of the apostles and prophets, Jesus Christ himself being the chief cornerstone, in whom the whole is joined together;[1] embracing as its members and subjects all the peculiar covenant people of God throughout the world;[2] and built up by Divine grace from age to age, as a habitation of God through the Spirit.[3]

[1] Col. i. 18; Eph. ii. 19-21. [2] Gen. xvii. 7; 1 Cor. xii. 12, 13; Acts ii. 39; Gal. iii. 9, 14. [3] Eph. ii. 21, 22; Rev. xxi. 3.

OF THE SACRAMENTS.

THE Lord Jesus Christ has instituted two sacraments, as holy signs and seals of the covenant of grace,[1] of the same spiritual signification as the corresponding sacraments of the Old Testament,[2] to be observed in the church until the end of the world,[3] namely, Baptism and the Lord's Supper;[4] the design of which is to represent Christ and his benefits, to confirm our interest in him, and solemnly to engage us to the service of God according to his word.[5]

[1] Gen. xvii. 7; Rom. iv. 11. [2] 1 Cor. x. 1-4; v. 7, 8. [3] Matt. xxviii. 19, 20; 1 Cor. xi. 26. [4] Matt. xxviii. 19; 1 Cor. xi. 23. [5] 1 Cor. x. 16; xi. 25, 26; Gal. iii. 27; Rom. vi. 3, 4.

OF BAPTISM.

BAPTISM is a sacrament of the New Testament, ordained by Christ,[1] to be unto the person baptized a sign and seal of the covenant of grace;[2] of his solemn admission into the visible church;[3] of the work of the Holy Spirit in renewing and sanctifying the heart;[4] and of his

[1] Matt. xxviii. 19. [2] Rom. iv. 11. [3] 1 Cor. xii. 13. [4] Titus iii. 5; Acts ii. 38.

obligation to walk in newness of life.[1] The proper subjects of the ordinance are professing believers and their households;[2] and it is rightly administered by sprinkling or pouring water upon the person, in the name of the Father, of the Son, and of the Holy Ghost.[3]

[1] Rom. vi. 3, 4. [2] Mark xvi. 15, 16; Gen. xvii. 7, 9; Acts ii. 38, 39; xvi. 14, 15, 33; 1 Cor. vii. 14; Mark x. 13, 14; Luke xviii. 15. [3] Acts x. 47; viii. 36; Matt. xxviii. 19; Heb. ix. 19; x. 22; Numb. viii. 7; Isaiah lii. 15; Ezek. xxxvi. 25; Zech. xii. 10; Isaiah xliv. 3; Joel ii. 28, 29.

OF THE LORD'S SUPPER.

THE Lord's Supper, consisting of bread and wine set apart from a common to a holy use by prayer,[1] was instituted by the Lord Jesus Christ,[2] as the sacrament of his body and blood,[3] to show forth perpetually the sacrifice of himself in his death;[4] to seal to believers the benefits of his atonement;[5] to promote the spiritual nourishment and growth of all who worthily receive it;[6] to be a bond of their communion with Christ and with each other, as members of his spiritual body;[7] and is to be administered to all who make a credible profession of evangelical faith, and maintain a blameless walk and conversation according to the Word of God.[8]

[1] Matt. xxvi. 26, 27. [2] 1 Cor. xi. 23-26. [3] 1 Cor. x. 16, 17, 21. [4] 1 Cor. xi. 24-27. [5] 2 Cor. i. 21, 22. [6] Eph. iv. 15, 16; ii. 21. [7] 1 Cor. x. 16, 17, 21; xii. 13. [8] 1 Cor. v. 6-8; xi. 27, 29; 2 Cor. vi. 14-16; 2 Thess. iii. 6, 14, 15.

OF THE CHRISTIAN SABBATH.

GOD has appointed one day in seven as a Sabbath to be kept holy unto him;[1] which, from the beginning

[1] Exodus xx. 8-11; Isaiah lvi. 2, 4, 6.

of the world to the resurrection of Christ, was the last day of the week,[1] and from the resurrection of Christ was changed into the first day of the week,[2] called in Scripture the Lord's day,[3] and is to be continued to the end of the world as the Christian Sabbath.[4]

[1] Gen. ii. 3. [2] 1 Cor. xvi. 1, 2; Acts xx. 7. [3] Rev. i. 10. [4] Exod. xx. 8, 10; Matt. v. 17, 18.

OF RELIGIOUS WORSHIP.

Religious worship, in the mode prescribed in the Scriptures,[1] is to be rendered unto God, the Father, Son, and Holy Ghost, and to him alone,[2] in the public and solemn assemblies of the saints on the Sabbath,[3] in secret,[4] and in private families daily;[5] with understanding,[6] faith,[7] love,[8] reverence, and godly fear;[9] through the mediation of Christ, our only redeemer and intercessor.[10]

[1] Deut. xii. 32; Matt. xv. 9. [2] Matt. iv. 10; John v. 23; Col. ii. 18. [3] Isaiah lvi. 7; Heb. x. 25; Acts ii. 42. [4] Matt. vi. 6; Eph. vi. 18. [5] Matt. vi. 11. [6] Psalm xlvii. 7. [7] James i. 6; Mark xi. 24. [8] Rev. ii. 4. [9] Heb. xii. 28. [10] John xiv. 6; 1 Tim. ii. 5.

OF THE COMMUNION OF SAINTS.

All the visible covenant people of God, being united to Jesus Christ their common head by faith,[1] and to each other by holy love,[2] are bound to maintain communion and fellowship in the worship and ordinances of God's house;[3] in the performance of such spiritual services as tend to their mutual edification;[4] and in relieving each others' necessities according to their ability and opportunity.[5]

[1] 1 John i. 3; Eph. iii. 16, 17. [2] Phil. ii. 1, 2; Eph. iv. 15, 16. [3] Heb. x. 24, 25; Acts ii. 42, 46. [4] Rom. xiv. 19; 1 Thess. v. 11. [5] 1 John iii. 17; Acts xi. 29, 30; Gal. vi. 10.

OF THE STATE OF MAN AFTER DEATH.

At death the bodies of men return to dust from which they were originally taken,[1] but their souls, which are immortal,[2] immediately return to God who gave them;[3] the righteous being received into heaven, where they behold the face of God in glory, waiting for the redemption of their bodies,[4] and the finally impenitent reserved in darkness unto the judgment to be punished.[5]

[1] Gen. iii. 19; Acts xiii. 36. [2] Gen. ii. 7; Matt. x. 28; Rev. xx. 4. [3] Luke xxiii. 43; Eccl. xii. 7. [4] Heb. xii. 23; Phil. i. 23; 1 John iii. 2; 2 Cor. v. 1-8. [5] Luke xvi. 23, 24; 2 Peter ii. 9.

OF THE RESURRECTION AND THE LAST JUDGMENT.

God hath appointed a day wherein he will raise the dead,[1] and judge the world in righteousness by Jesus Christ, to whom all power and judgment belong;[2] when all, who have lived upon the earth, shall appear before his tribunal to give an account of the deeds done in the body, and to receive according to what they have done, whether it be good or evil;[3] then the righteous, being made perfect in holiness, and united to bodies fashioned like unto Christ's glorious body,[4] will enter into eternal life and blessedness;[5] and the wicked, receiving bodies raised to dishonor,[6] will be punished with everlasting destruction from the presence of the Lord, and from the glory of his power.[7]

[1] Acts xxiv. 15; John v. 28, 29; 1 Cor. xv. 12-21.
[2] Acts xvii. 31; John v. 22, 27.
[3] 2 Cor. v. 10; Eccl. xii. 14; Matt. xii. 36, 37; Rom. ii. 16; Rev. xx. 12.
[4] Phil. iii. 21; 1 Cor. xv. 42-49.
[5] Matt. xxv. 31-34; Rom. ii. 7; Luke xx. 36; Rev. xx. 6.
[6] Daniel xii. 2.
[7] Rom. ii. 5, 6; 2 Thess. i. 7, 8; Matt. xxv. 41, 46; Rev. xx. 15.

PRACTICAL RULES

FOR THE DIRECTION OF THE CONSCIENCE.

"That the man of God may be perfect, thoroughly furnished unto all good works."

PRACTICAL RULES.

I. Maintain, according to your ability and opportunity, all the ordinances which Christ has instituted for his own glory, and the edification of the Church.

II. Regard the favor and everlasting enjoyment of God as the great end of life, and let all your plans and efforts in the world have primary reference to this end.

III. Contemplate the obedience, sacrifice, mediation, and intercession of Christ, as the procuring cause of all blessings, temporal, spiritual, and eternal; and gratefully acknowledge him as the only source of your peace and joy.

IV. Earnestly strive to walk in Christ's steps, and to be holy as he is holy, that you may adorn the doctrine of God your Saviour in all things, and recommend the religion of the gospel to the consciences and hearts of your fellow-men.

V. Ever keep in mind that love to God and zeal for his glory are the highest duties of the Christian; and judge of your acceptable performance of them, not by occasional excitement, but by your habitual frame of mind; by the punctual and steady discharge of the obligations which rest upon you as Christians; by your cheerful submission to the divine will; and by your constant and earnest efforts to promote the kingdom of Christ in the world.

VI. Remember the Sabbath day to keep it holy according to the commandment; and endeavor to avoid all disturbance and wandering of mind in the services of the sanctuary; to banish worldly cares from the heart, and exclude secular subjects from conversation on the Lord's day; and to make it a season of sacred rest and of holy enjoyment.

VII. Maintain the daily worship of God in the family and in the closet; and that you may avoid all coldness and formality in this service, prepare yourselves for it by devout reading and meditation.

VIII. Set apart convenient and sufficient seasons for a prayerful, systematic, and thorough study of the Bible, that you may grow in knowledge and in spiritual understanding of divine truth; that you may be able to serve and worship God according to his will; that you may not be tossed to and fro, and blown about by every wind of doctrine; and that you may be perfectly joined together in the same judgment respecting the essential doctrines and duties of religion.

IX. Guard against a selfish and exclusive devotion to your own interests, and endeavor in all suitable ways to promote the well-being of your fellow-men.

X. Cultivate a kind and benignant temper towards all, and strive to avoid everything that will tend unnecessarily to wound the character or feelings of others.

XI. Make it your great object to understand clearly, and to perform faithfully, all the duties resulting from your several relations as men and as Christians.

XII. Frequently review the solemn Covenant which you have entered into with God and his people, and study to reform whatever has been wrong in your temper or conduct, and to bring your whole inward and outward life into harmony with what you have publicly engaged to do, relying upon the atoning merits of your crucified Redeemer for pardon and acceptance, and upon the sanctifying influence of the Holy Spirit for growth in grace, and complete victory over sin.

XIII. Finally,—Whatsoever things are true, whatsoever things are honest, whatsoever things are just, whatsoever things are pure, whatsoever things are lovely, whatsoever things are of good report; if there be any virtue, and if there be any praise, think on these things.

And the peace of God, which passeth knowledge, shall keep your hearts and minds through Christ Jesus.

ECCLESIASTICAL PRINCIPLES.

AND

STANDING RULES.

For though I be absent in the flesh, yet am I with you in the spirit, joying and beholding your ORDER, and the steadfastness of your faith in Christ."

The form of Government adopted by this Church is that set forth in the "Cambridge Platform," agreed upon by the Elders and Messengers of the Churches assembled in the Synod at Cambridge, 1648, from which the following Principles are in substance selected, for the benefit of those members who have not access to the original work.

ECCLESIASTICAL PRINCIPLES.

CHURCH GOVERNMENT.

Ecclesiastical polity, or church government, is that form and order which Christ has required to be observed in his church upon earth, both as to its constitution and all the ordinances which are administered in it.

NATURE OF THE CHRISTIAN CHURCH.

The Christian church is a spiritual kingdom, of which Jesus Christ is the supreme head and lawgiver, embracing all who are described in the Scriptures as the covenant people of God, throughout the world.

A CONGREGATIONAL CHURCH.

A Congregational church is a portion of the visible church, consisting of a convenient number of visible believers, united in one body by a holy covenant, submitting to a Scriptural form of government, and meeting together in one place for the worship of God; for the regular administration of the sacraments of the gospel; for the exercise of discipline; and for their mutual edification in the knowledge and fellowship of the gospel.

RIGHTS OF THE CHURCH.

Every particular church is a complete body in itself, and has authority to adopt that form of government which appears most agreeable to the Word of God; to manage its internal affairs; to choose those officers whom Christ has designated and ordained to teach and rule in the Church; to regulate the admission, discipline, and removal of its own members, according to the rule laid down in the Scriptures; and is amenable to no ecclesiastical power upon earth, except by its own consent, or agreeably to the established usage of Congregational churches.

PERMANENT OFFICERS.

The ordinary and permanent officers of the church are Pastors and Deacons; who are to be regularly chosen and called by the particular church in which they are to minister, and, after thorough examination in respect to their fitness for the work to which they are called, to be ordained according to the mode approved and in use in Congregational churches.

DUTIES OF PASTORS.

It belongs to the office of Pastor to take the oversight of the church in respect to spiritual things; to preach the Word; to administer the seals of the Covenant; to pronounce the sentence of the church upon offenders; to call the church together upon necessary occasions; to preside in all church meetings; and, finally, to labor in all appointed ways "for the perfecting of the saints, and the edifying of the body of Christ, until they come in the unity of the faith, and the knowledge of the Son of God, unto a perfect man, unto the measure of the stature of the fullness of Christ."

DUTIES OF DEACONS.

THE duty of the Deacons is to receive and keep the funds of the church; to provide the necessary elements for the proper administration of the sacraments; to apply such portion of the funds in their hands as the church may direct to the relief of the poor; and in the absence of the Pastor, to preside in the meetings of the church in rotation.

DUTY OF THE CHURCH TOWARDS ITS OFFICERS.

ALTHOUGH churches cannot be compelled to receive any officer not freely chosen by themselves, yet when a fit person is regularly ordained over them by their own choice and consent, they are bound to submit to the authority with which he is invested by the Head of the Church, and to esteem him very highly in love for his work's sake.

MAINTENANCE OF PASTORS.

IT is the duty of the church to furnish a suitable and sufficient maintenance to those who are called to labor in word and doctrine, not as matter of alms, but of debt, that they may give themselves wholly to the work of the ministry, without embarrassment in respect to their temporal support.

IMPORTANCE OF A PUBLIC PROFESSION.

ALL believers ought to join themselves, if possible, to some particular church, that they may honor the Lord Jesus Christ by a public profession of their faith, and subjection to the order and ordinances of the gospel; that they may have fellowship with the visible people of God in their work and privileges; that they and their children may receive the promises made to the Church; and that they may be instrumental in promoting and perpetuating the visible kingdom of God upon earth.

ADMISSION OF MEMBERS.

When a person wishes to join himself to the church, he should make known his desire to the pastor, or one of the deacons if the church is destitute of a pastor, and if there be no objection, he is at some convenient time to be examined by the pastor and a committee of the church, as to his repentance towards God, his faith in the Lord Jesus Christ, his acquaintance with the doctrines and usages of the church, and his preparation to perform the duties and enjoy the privileges of a church member; and then, if the examination is satisfactory, he is to be propounded to the church a reasonable time before his admission, that the members may be prepared to receive him as becometh saints.

If any member of the church feels seriously dissatisfied with the character or conduct of a person propounded for admission, he should first endeavor to obtain satisfaction by a private interview with the candidate; or, failing in this, he should state the ground of his dissatisfaction to the pastor, or to one of the examining committee, and to no other person, that suitable measures may be taken to remove the difficulty, and preserve the peace and purity of the church.

REMOVAL OF MEMBERS.

No member may withdraw from the communion and fellowship of the church in the worship and ordinances of the gospel without just and weighty cause; nor can any one cease to be under the watch, care, and discipline of the church, except by excommunication for a violation of covenant, or by dismission and recommendation to some other church.

If a member has occasion to remove for a season to another place where there is a sister church, letters of recommendation are requisite and sufficient for communion with that church in the ordinances of the gospel.

When a member wishes to remove permanently from one church to another, it is his duty to ask for a letter of dismission and recommendation, stating the grounds of his request, which the church is bound to grant, unless the removal be manifestly unsafe or sinful; and any other mode of withdrawing from the church is disorderly and just ground of censure.

RIGHTS OF MEMBERS.

Every member of the church is entitled to all its privileges, until they are forfeited by unchristian conduct; and when thus forfeited, he can be deprived of them only by regular process of discipline.

CHURCH DISCIPLINE.

It is the duty of the church to maintain that discipline which Christ has appointed; for the removal of offences, for the vindication of the honor of religion, for the purification and edification of the church, for the restoration of offending members, and for the purpose of averting the displeasure of God, which may justly be manifested towards a church that suffers the ordinances of religion to be profaned by obstinate offenders.

PRIVATE OFFENCES.

In all cases of private and personal offences, the offender is to be dealt with in the mode pointed out by Christ, Matt.

xviii. 15, 16; and no complaint, or information, in respect to such offences, can be admitted by the church, until the means of reconciliation and of reclaiming the offender, there required, have been faithfully employed. If a person gives publicity to a private offence, except in pursuing the regular course of discipline, or in the discharge of some other indispensable duty, he sins against his brother, and is liable to the censure of the church.

PUBLIC OFFENCES.

When an offence is at first public, and of a heinous and scandalous nature, the previous steps pointed out in case of private offences need not be taken; but the church, upon a proper complaint, may take immediate cognizance of it. It is, however, in most cases admissible for some brother, or a committee of the church, first to converse privately with the accused.

PROCESS OF DISCIPLINE.

When a member is complained of before the church, he is entitled to due notice of the precise sin or sins with which he is charged, to a reasonable time for preparing his defence, and to an open and impartial hearing; and no vote of censure can be lawfully passed by the church, except by the concurrence of a majority, at a regular meeting expressly notified for that purpose.

CHURCH CENSURES.

If a person, when proved guilty of an offence by competent testimony, does not give satisfaction to the church by a penitent confession, he is to be admonished, publicly or privately, excluded from the enjoyment of church privileges, or cast out of the church by excommunication, according to the nature and aggravation of his sin. If the sentence of the church is followed by the humble confession, repentance, and obvious amendment of the offender, he is to be forgiven, comforted, and restored to his former standing in the church.

FELLOWSHIP OF CHURCHES.

All those churches which have obtained "like precious faith through the righteousness of God and our Saviour Jesus Christ," and hold the same Divine Head, though distinct, ought to maintain communion and fellowship, by extending to each other the privilege of communion at the Lord's Table; by the mutual transfer of members when circumstances render removal expedient; by the occasional exchange of pastoral services; by giving and receiving advice and assistance through mutual councils, agreeably to the established usage of Congregational churches; and by earnest efforts to promote each other's welfare.

To these Ecclesiastical Principles the following is added upon the

OBLIGATIONS OF MEMBERS.

Every member of a church is under obligation to be loyal to the church with which he is connected, and to prove his devotion by liberally supporting the church in its work, with money and effort, by diligent attendance upon its services, by promoting a spirit of fellowship among its members, by advancing its interests and influence in the community by all proper means, and by so increasing his own piety as to enlarge its efficiency and gain for it the approval of the Great Head of the Church.

STANDING RULES.

---

1. All meetings of the church shall be opened with prayer.

2. The annual meeting for the choice of officers, and the transaction of other business, shall be in January; the time to be appointed by the pastor and deacons, and notice to be given from the pulpit on the Sabbath preceding.

3. There shall be a committee of the church, consisting of the pastor, the deacons, the clerk of the church, the superintendent of the Sabbath-school, and two other brethren to be chosen by ballot at the annual meeting. This committee shall examine candidates for admission to the church, and propound such persons as they approve. This committee shall also act as a Board of Advice in matters relating to the church.

4. Candidates for admission, whether by letter or profession, shall be propounded first to the church, and notice thereof be given to the congregation, at least two weeks previous to their admission.

5. At the close of every Preparatory Lecture there shall be a stated church meeting, at which the vote in relation to the admission of candidates shall be taken.

6. All persons admitted to the church shall be required to sign our Confession of Faith, Covenant, and Rules.

7. The Sacrament of the Lord's Supper is administered once in two months, upon the first Sabbaths in January, March, May, July, September, and November.

8. Those who join the church by profession shall be admitted in the presence of the congregation, after the sermon, on the day of the administration of the Lord's Supper.

9. Members of the church who are about to remove from town are expected to make known their intention to the pastor, and receive letters of recommendation to the church, if there be one in fellowship with us, in the place to which they are going.

10. Members of other churches who are permanently settled in this place, and desire to walk in fellowship with this church, are expected to obtain a removal of their church relationship to us as soon as they conveniently can, unless they assign a satisfactory reason for delay to the pastor.

11. All applications for letters of dismission and recommendation shall be made in writing, stating the ground upon which they are desired.

12. The church shall meet on Friday evenings for devotional exercises and religious conference.

13. Any alteration may be made in these Rules, at a regular church meeting called for the purpose, or at the annual meeting of the church.

CONFESSION AND COVENANT.

"That He would grant you, according to the riches of his glory, to be strengthened with might by his Spirit in the inner man; that Christ may dwell in your hearts by faith."

FORM OF ADMISSION

TO THE

COMMUNION OF THE CHURCH.

The Candidates shall present themselves before the Pulpit, where they shall be met by the Minister, who shall repeat one or more of the following sentences of the Holy Scriptures, or such other sentences as he may choose: —

Come unto Me, all ye that labor and are heavy laden, and I will give you rest. Take my yoke upon you, and learn of Me; for I am meek and lowly in heart; and ye shall find rest unto your souls. For my yoke is easy, and my burden is light.

And the Spirit and the Bride say, Come. And let him that heareth say, Come. And let him that is athirst come. And whosoever will, let him take the water of life freely.

Whosoever therefore shall confess Me before men, him will I confess also before my Father which is in heaven.

The Minister shall then address the Candidates as follows, and shall recite the Creed of the church for their assent: —

Dearly Beloved, — You have presented yourselves in this holy place to make confession of the Lord Jesus Christ, and to enter into covenant with his Church. We trust that you know the solemnity and the blessedness of this time, and we are confident that He which hath begun a good work in you will perform it until the day of Jesus Christ.

WE BELIEVE in one living and true GOD; Creator,

Preserver, and Ruler of all things: glorious in holiness, plenteous in mercy and truth.

In the FATHER ALMIGHTY: Lord and giver of life; who is to be supremely loved and perfectly obeyed; whose commandment is holy and just and good.

And in JESUS CHRIST, HIS SON, OUR LORD; who was in the beginning with God and was God; who for us men, and for our salvation, came down from heaven and was made man. He was crucified, dead, and buried. He arose from the dead and ascended into heaven, and sitteth on the right hand of the FATHER. He shall come again with glory to judge both the quick and the dead; when every one shall receive the things done in his body, according to that he hath done, whether it be good or bad. Of His kingdom there shall be no end.

And we BELIEVE in the HOLY GHOST, the COMFORTER; by whom the Scriptures were given: who renews and sanctifies the heart; by whose power we are kept unto immortal life. Who, with the FATHER and the SON, together ONE GOD, is to be worshipped and glorified, world without end.

Before ALMIGHTY GOD our HEAVENLY FATHER, we humbly acknowledge our guiltiness, casting ourselves upon His infinite goodness and mercy.

We BELIEVE in the forgiveness of sins through our Lord and Saviour Jesus Christ, whose name we confess, whose Word we receive, in whose mediation alone we steadfastly trust.

We BELIEVE in one Church, on earth and in heaven: in one Baptism: in one Communion in the body and blood of Christ; and we look for the Resurrection of the dead, and the Life of the world to come. Amen.

You who have now made this Confession do acknowledge the Lord Jehovah — the FATHER, the SON, and the HOLY GHOST — to be your God; to Him you devote your supreme affection; to His service you consecrate your lives; and naming yourself with the name of Christ, you avow your purpose to glorify Him in your body and in your spirit, which are His.

Baptism will here be administered to those who have not before been baptized, with these words, —

A. B., I baptize thee, in the name of the FATHER, and of the SON, and of the HOLY GHOST. Amen.

To the other Candidates the Minister shall say, —

You who were baptized in childhood do now gratefully accept that as your baptism, while you confirm the covenant which then was made for you.

The Members of the Church shall here rise and the Minister shall continue: —

Because you make this Confession, We, the members of this Church, affectionately welcome you to fellowship with us in all duties and blessings, rejoicing with you in the joy of the Lord, and praying for you with assurance and longing, that when the Chief Shepherd shall appear, ye may receive a crown of glory that fadeth not away.

Here the Church, with those who have just made confession, and those who have been received from other churches, shall repeat this covenant, saying: —

We who are now brought together and united into one Church, under the Lord Jesus Christ, our Head, in such sort as becometh all those whom He hath redeemed and sanctified to Himself, do here solemnly and religiously, as in His most holy presence, promise and bind ourselves to walk in all our ways according to the rule of the Gospel, and in all sincere conformity to His holy ordinances, and in mutual love and respect each to other, so near as God shall give us grace.

Here the Minister shall take the new members by the hand in token of fellowship with Christ and the Church, repeating some appropriate sentence of Scripture. He shall then address them in these words: —

Now, therefore, Beloved in the Lord, ye are no more strangers and foreigners, but fellow-citizens with the saints, and of the household of God; and are built upon the foundation of the Apostles and Prophets, Jesus Christ Himself being the chief Corner-stone. For this cause —

[Here all will take the customary attitude of prayer]

we bow our knees unto the Father of our Lord Jesus Christ, of whom the whole family in heaven and earth is named, that He would grant you, according to the riches of His glory, to be strengthened with might by His Spirit in the inner man; that Christ may dwell in your hearts by faith; that ye, being rooted and grounded in love, may be able to comprehend with all saints, what is the breadth, and length, and depth, and height, and to know the love of Christ which passeth knowledge, that ye might be filled with all the fulness of God.

Now unto Him that is able to do exceeding abundantly above all that we ask or think, according to the power that worketh in us, unto Him be glory in the Church by Christ Jesus throughout all ages, world without end. Amen.

PRESENT OFFICERS OF THE CHURCH,

WITH THE

NAMES OF MEMBERS,

BEGINNING WITH ITS FORMATION.

PRESENT OFFICERS OF THE CHURCH.

1872.

PASTOR.

REV. ALEXANDER McKENZIE.

DEACONS.

STEPHEN T. FARWELL, CHARLES W. HOMER,
GEORGE S. SAUNDERS.

CLERK.

G. S. SAUNDERS.

STANDING COMMITTEE.

The Standing Committee of the Church consists of the Pastor, Deacons, the Clerk, Superintendent of the Sabbath School (FRANCIS FLINT), and the following Brethren: —

CHARLES W. MUNROE, JAMES A. SHEDD.

CATALOGUE

OF THE

OFFICERS AND MEMBERS OF THE CHURCH.

PASTORS.

Rev. THOMAS SHEPARD, ordained February, 1636. Died August 25, 1649.

Rev. JONATHAN MITCHELL, ordained August 21, 1650. Died July 9, 1668.

Rev. URIAN OAKES, ordained November 8, 1671. Died July 25, 1681.

Rev. NATHANIEL GOOKIN, ordained November 15, 1682. Died August 7, 1692.

Rev. WILLIAM BRATTLE, ordained November 25, 1696. Died February 15, 1717.

Rev. NATHANIEL APPLETON, D. D., ordained October 9, 1717. Died February 9, 1784.

Rev. TIMOTHY HILLIARD, installed October 27, 1783. Died May 9, 1790.

Rev. ABIEL HOLMES, D. D., installed January 25, 1792. Dismissed September 26, 1831.

Rev. NEHEMIAH ADAMS, ordained December 17, 1829. Dismissed March 14, 1834.

Rev. JOHN A. ALBRO, D. D., installed April 15, 1835. Dismissed April 15, 1865.

Rev. ALEXANDER McKENZIE, installed January 24, 1867.

RULING ELDERS.

[The following List comprises the names of those who are known to have been Ruling Elders of the Church.]

Edmund Frost. He came to New England in 1635, and was made a Freeman in 1636. He died July 12, 1672.

Richard Champney. He came to New England in 1635, and was made a Freeman in 1636. He died November 26, 1669.

Jonas Clark. He was made a Freeman in 1647. Ordained Ruling Elder November 15, 1682. He died January 11, 1699, aged eighty years.

John Stone. He came to New England in 1635, it is thought, and was made a Freeman in 1665. Ordained Ruling Elder November 15, 1682. He died May 5, 1683, aged sixty-four years.

DEACONS.

[The following List comprises the names of those who are known to have been Deacons of the Church.]

JOHN BRIDGE. Freeman 1635. Died 1665.
THOMAS MARRIOT. Freeman 1636. Died 1664.
THOMAS CHEESEHOLME. Freeman 1636. Died 1671.
GREGORY STONE. Freeman 1636. Died 1672.
NATHANIEL SPARROWHAWKE. Freeman 1639. Died 1647.
NATHANIEL SPARROWHAWKE. Freeman. Died January, 1687.
EDWARD COLLINS. Freeman 1640. Died 1689.
JOHN COOPER. Freeman 1642. Died 1691.
WALTER HASTING. Born 1631. Died 1705.
SAMUEL COOPER. Chosen March 22, 1705. Died 1718.
NATHANIEL HANCOCK. Chosen June 7, 1705. Died 1719.
SAMUEL KIDDER. Chosen January 22, 1718. Died 1724.
JOSEPH COOLIDGE. Chosen January 22, 1718. Died 1737.
NATHANIEL SPARROWHAWKE. Chosen August 5, 1724. Died 1734.
SAMUEL BOWMAN. Chosen August 5, 1724. Died before 1741.
SAMUEL SPARROWHAWKE. Chosen April 12, 1734. Died 1774.
JOHN BRADISH. Chosen May 5, 1738. Died 1741.
SAMUEL WHITTEMORE. Chosen November 24, 1741. Died about 1783.
HENRY PRENTICE. Chosen November 24, 1741. Resigned July 14, 1774.
AARON HILL. Chosen July 14, 1774. Died 1792.
STEPHEN SEWALL. Chosen May 18, 1777. Died 1804.
GIDEON FROST. Chosen June 30, 1783. Died 1803.
JAMES MUNROE. Chosen June 30, 1783. Died 1804.
JOHN WALTON. Chosen November 19, 1792. Died 1823.
WILLIAM HILLIARD. Chosen April 5, 1804. Died 1836.
JOSIAH MOORE. Chosen January 4, 1805. Died 1814.
JAMES MUNROE. Chosen August 2, 1818. Died 1848.
STEPHEN T. FARWELL. Installed April 30, 1837.
CHARLES W. HOMER. Installed January 4, 1849.
CHARLES THEO. RUSSELL. Installed July 2, 1869.
GEORGE S. SAUNDERS. Installed July 2, 1869.

PERSONS WHO OWNED THE COVENANT IN ORDER TO THEIR CHILDREN'S BEING BAPTIZED.

1696.
Nathaniel Sparrowhawke and wife,
Daniel Champney and wife,
William Barrett and wife,
John Squire, Jun., and wife.

1697.
Samuel Champney,
Jonathan Nutting and wife,
Wife of Abraham Hill,
Samuel Sparrowhawke,
Thomas Prentice.

1698.
Wife of Josiah Parker,
Ebenezer Brooks, of Mystic,
Wife of John Kent,
Percival Hall, of Medford.

1699.
Ebenezer Swan,
Jonathan Butterfield and wife,
John Fillebrown and wife,
Widow Hannah Hasting.

1700.
Stephen Frost,
Abraham Ireland and wife,
John Streeter.

1701.
William Patten,
Paul Bat.

1702.
Daniel Hasting,
Nathaniel Patten.

1703.
Andrew Wilson and wife.

1704.
Wife of Stephen Coolidge,
John Fessenden,
Wife of Ebenezer Hancock.

1706.
Jonathan Hyde,
Walter Russell.

1707.
Rebeccah Barrett,
John Whitmore, Jun., of Medford.

1708.
Lydia Davis, of Boston,
Jonathan Robinson and wife,
Samuel Robins and wife,
Sarah Lewis [restored].

1709.
Gershom Davis and wife,
James Holding.

1710.
Joseph Robins,
William Willis,
Elizabeth Humphreys.

1711.
Hubbert Russell,
Joshua Gammage,
Daniel Squire,
Aaron Bordman,
Goody Mullet,
Joseph Adams.

1712.
Isaac Watson,
John Green.

1713.
Nathaniel Prentice,
Jonathan Gates,
Samuel Angier,
Thomas Harrington,
Nathaniel Cutter.

1714.
Nathaniel Winship,
Jonathan Wyeth,
Thomas Fillebrown,
George Abbot.

1716.
John Parker,
William Winship, Jun.,
Daniel Gookin.

1719.
John Swan,
William Dickson,
John Winship,
Henry Prentice and wife,
Elizabeth Prentice,
Thomas Dana.

1720.
Edward Manning,
John Phillips, of Watertown.

1721.
Jonathan Shattuck, of Watertown,
Eleazer Parker,
Samuel Cutter,
Joseph Shed,
Samuel Whittemore, of Charlestown.

1722.
John Gale,
John Chadwick, of Watertown,
Jemima Baverick,
Jonathan Bradshaw.

1723.
Charles Honeywell,
Elizabeth Wheat,
Ebenezer Cutter,
Thomas Brown,
Joseph Winship.

1724.
Nathaniel Francis,
Ebenezer Frost,
John Fessenden, Jun.,
Peter Tufts,
James Tufts,
Ebenezer Shed,
Jabez Carter, of Woburn,
Isaac Fillebrown and wife,
Hannah Fillebrown,
Thomas Soden.

1725.
Noah Sparrowhawke.

1726.
Andrew Wilson,
John Dickson, Jun.,
Benjamin Brasier,
Samuel Cook, Jun.

1727.
Caleb Dana,
Benjamin Emms and wife,
Edward Russell and wife.

1728.
Luxford Patten,
Ephraim Cook,
James Ozborn.

1729.
Henry Carnel.

1730.
George Cutter,
Ebenezer Swan and wife,
John Wilson.

1731.
Andrew Bordman, Jun.

1733.
Samuel Bull,
Jacob Hill, Jun.

1734.
Samuel Goddin,
James Thompson,
Nathaniel Gammage.

1735.
Thomas Ozborn.

1736.
Samuel Hastings,
Simon Holding and wife,
Samuel Lock,
William Withington.

1737.
Wife of Simon Sparrowhawke,
Abraham Ireland,
Samuel Davis,
Samuel Swan.

1738.
Wife of Abraham Colfry,
Mary Parker,
Daniel Barrett,
Tabitha Skinner.

1739.
Wife of Nathaniel Chadwick,
Angus Graham,
Tabitha Hill.

1740.
Ebenezer Bradish,
Ebenezer Smith.

1741.
Samuel Champney, Jun.

1742.
Elias Mason,
Josiah Crosbye,
John Cheney,
Martha Cheney,
Daniel Smith.

1743.
Elizabeth Hinds.

1744.
Wife of James Lanman,
David Logan.

1746.
Abraham Cutting,
Priscilla Cutting.

1747.
Daniel Champney, Jun.,
Nathan Winchester, Brookline,
Joseph Cook, Jun.,
Edward Manning, Jun.,
Edward Thwing and wife.

1748.
Abraham Frost,
Henry Coolidge,
John Hicks,
Stephen Stearns.

1749.
John Dickson, Jun.,
John Ellis, Jun., B. A.

1752.
Abraham Watson, Jun.,
Martha Hubbard.

1753.
Elisha Hagar and wife,
William How,
William Bordman,
Joseph Brown,
Mary Randall,
Nathaniel Sparrowhawke and wife.

1754.
Jonas Wyeth,
Gideon Frost,
Wife of Michael Gill,
James Frost and wife,
Peleg Stearns,
Jonas Larned.

1755.
Daniel Dana,
Samuel Thatcher, Jun.,
John Warland,
Ebenezer Brown.

1756.
Jonathan Cooper, Jun.,
David Larned,
Thomas Gardner.

1757.
Solomon Champney, Jun., and wife,
Caleb Dana, Jun.,
Henry Holden.

1758.
David Smith.

1759.
John Thwing,
Daniel Watson,
William Honeywell, Jun.

1760.
Samuel Choate,
Thomas Mayo,
Samuel Chandler,
James Bryant,
Jedediah Larned and wife,
Bethiah Champney.

1761.
Elizabeth Dolly,
Benjamin Hill and wife,
Joseph Allen,
John Kidder and wife.

1762.
John Nutting,
Amos Marrett,
Samuel Gookin, Jun.,
Mary Durant.

1763.
William Bowles,
Elisha Holmes,
James Ballard,
Noah Wyeth and wife.

1764.
Thomas Hovey,
Jonathan Dana,
Christopher Grant, Jun., and wife,
Wife of Nathaniel Tufts,
Robert Twadell,
William Darling,
Thomas Thwing, Jun., and his wife,
Simon Howard,
Richard Dana,
Mary Barrett,
Ebenezer Sever,
James Kettle,
John Barret and wife,
Wife of Samuel Hill.

1765.
Richard Honeywell,
Joshua Converse and wife,
Jonathan Fessenden and wife,
Samuel Fessenden and wife,
Jacob Watson,
William Tufts.

1766.
Joseph Miller,
Downing Champney,
Nathaniel Prentice,
James Holton.

1767.
Edward Richards and wife,
Joel Fisk and wife,
Zechariah Shed,
Henry Dickson,
Widow Elizabeth Cook.

1768.
Nathaniel Jarvis and wife,
Timothy Koree and wife,
John Wyman and wife,
Joshua Lee and wife,
Josiah Moore and wife.

1769.
Nathaniel Robbins,
Jonathan Winship and wife,
Josiah Fessenden and wife,
Aaron Tufts and wife.

1770.
Stephen Goddard and wife,
John Caldwell and wife,
Ephraim Hammond and wife,
Walter Cox,
Thomas Philips,
Stephen Read and wife.

1771.
Edward Fillebrown,
Widow Rebeccah Pratt,
Nathaniel Thwing and wife,
Anne, a negro woman of Jonathan Hastings, Esq.

1772.
Isaac Trask,
William Hunt,
Moses Griggs and wife,
Benaiah Davenport and wife,
Joseph Bates,
Thomas Barret,
John Butterfield.

1773.
John Prentice,

Samuel Champney and wife,
Jonathan Butterfield,
James Read and wife,
Caleb Rand.

1774.
Jotham Walton,
George Douglass and wife.

1775.
Stephen Palmer, Jun., and his wife,
Torrey Hancock and wife,
David Comee and wife.

1776.
Samuel Butterfield,
Jonathan Ireland,
Thomas Prentiss,
John Warland,
John Rice and wife.

1777.
Susannah Morse,
Isaiah Dickson,
Benjamin Myrick and wife,
Henry Coolidge,
Jesse Putnam, B. A.

1778.
Samuel Phipps,
Daniel Swan,
Ebenezer Wyeth, Jun.,
Samuel Manning,
Joshua Gammage,
Jonathan Temple,
George Geyer and wife,
Dr. William Gammage, Jun.,
Joseph Holden,
Thomas Fillebrown.

1780.
William Watson,
John Hastings.

1782.
Jabez Frothingham,
Amos Briant,
John Palmer,
William Honeywell and wife.

1783.
Richard Cutter, Jun.,
Thomas Warland,
Joshua Stacey Reed,
Major John Hastings.

1784.
Samuel Babcock.

1786.
Samuel Townsend.

1787.
Ebenezer Stedman,
Widow Elizabeth Frost,
Thomas Rand.

1788.
John Shed,
Elisha Doane.

1789.
Betsey Nelson,
Andrew Lopans,
Jonathan Wyatt,
Katherine Smith.

1792.
Rayham Richardson and wife,
Walter Frost.

1793.
Joshua Palmer,
Asa Moore,
Reuben and Henrietta Moore,
Samuel Cox,
Joseph Sawing,
Elizabeth Wyeth.

1794.
Samuel Choate,
Jacob Page,
Isaac Tapley.

1795.
Scarborough Parker,
Thomas Miller,
Joshua Chamberlin,
Thezia Mills.

1796.
George Bonner,
Jonathan Butterfield,
Adino Hastings,
William and Ruth Bradish.

1797.
Walter and Susanna Cox,
Nathaniel Prentiss Watson.

1798.
Robert Vose,
Samuel Locke, Jun.,
Isaac Tufts.

1799.
Samuel, Jr., and Hannah Tufts,
Jacob Murdock,
James and Anna Adams,
Jonas and Mary Fillebrown.

1800.
Sarah Flagg,
Richard and Abigail Thayer,
Nathaniel and Susanna Faulkner,
Lemuel and Elizabeth King,
Jacob, Jr., and Abigail Watson.

1801.
Samuel and Elizabeth Child,
Oliver Blake,
John and Judith Heyden,
Aaron and Lydia Parker.

1802.
John Cutter Stone and Eliza Stone.

1803.
Artenatus and Sukey Moore,
Samuel and Martha Gould.

1804.
Samuel Flagg Sawyer,
Nathaniel and Martha Munro,
Benjamin and Betsey Grover,
Nathan and Hannah Barns.

1805.
Job and Lydia Converse Wyeth,
Joshua and Abigail Sawing,
Solomon and Susanna Hancock,
Cyrus and Deborah French.

1806.
John Cook,
Joseph Holmes,
Lemuel and Sarah Brackett,
John, Jr., and Sarah Warland,
Luke and Susanna H. Pool,
Jabez and Lucy Whiting,
William Russell,
Jason Howe.

1807.
Torrey and Olive Hancock,
Chester and Sarah Sessions,
John Tarbell,
Franklin and Mary Sawyer.

1808.
Jonas and Ellen Prentiss,
Abraham Watson Gammage.

1809.
Thomas and Martha Austin.

1810.
Eliab Wight Metcalf,
Lydia Metcalf,
William and Anne Hunnewell,
Joseph and Lydia Beers.

1813.
Jonathan and Elizabeth Gary,
Jonathan C. and Mary Prentiss,
John Hutcherson Learned and wife.

1814.
William and Mary Warland,
Artemas Putnam,
Mehetable Putnam.

1817.
Amos and Hannah Teal.

1818.
Loammi and Ann Baldwin.

1822.
Henry and Abigail Nowell.

1824.
Asa and Susan Cutter.

1825.
Josiah Nottage Marshall,
Elizabeth Marshall.

1828.
Jonathan and Experience Hyde.

PERSONS ADULT WHO OWNED THE COVENANT AND WERE BAPTIZED.

1696.

Isaac Knap,
Arthur Cole,
John Oldham, Jun.,
Dorothy Hancock,
Hannah Minot,
Jane Matson,
Abigail Oldham,
Margaret Agar,
Sarah Lewis,
Stephen Palmer,
Mercy Makoon,
Deliverance Ferguson,
Susanna Homan,
Mercy Agar,
Elizabeth Lyn,
Priscilla Lyn,
Sarah Batson,
Elizabeth Trane,
Abigail Trane,
Abigail Knap.

1697.

Abraham Hill,
Nathaniel Batson.

1698.

Joseph Crackbone,
Sarah Crackbone,
Philip, a negro servant of Mr. Danforth.

1700.

Richard Cutter and his sister,
Elizabeth Cutter,
Ebenezer Redding,
Lydia Cutter,
Hannah Cutter.

1701.

William Delloway,
Mary Delloway,
Elizabeth Cookworthy.

1702.

Gershom Cutter.

1704.

Mrs. Blower,
Wife of John Knight,
Hannah Francis,
Lydia Pierce,
Joseph Hovey,
Caleb Hovey.

1705.

Mingo and Charles, negro servants of Mr. Town,
Jeffrey, a negro servant of Mr. Goff,
Scipio, a servant,
Abigail, wife of John Robins,
Mary, wife of John Prentice,
Elizabeth Burges.

1707.

Henry Dunster,
Isabell Cutter, daughter of Gershom Cutter,
Nathaniel Clark.

1708.

Anna Furbush.

1711.

Aaron Cleveland,
Mary Fowl.

1712.

William Burges,
Mercy Jones,
Jason Williams,
John Williams,
Nathaniel Williams,
Jacob Green,
John Burges.

1715.

Cornelius Nye, a student,
Elizabeth Durant.

1718.

Miriam Cheever,

Elizabeth Ence,
Margaret Williams.

1719.
Elizabeth Sangor,
Hannah Colson,
Mindwell Palks,
Consider Lycore.

1720.
Ebenezer Burgess.

1721.
Hannah Daniels, Jun.,
Peter Hurd.

1722.
Judah Monis,
Thomas Robins,
Thomas Crossen,
Deborah Crossen,
Elizabeth Baverick.

1723.
Jonathan Dunster,
Thomas Dunster,
David Dunster,
Elizabeth Dunster,
Dorothy Dunster,
John Baverick,
Ruth Baverick.

1724.
Mary Redeford.

1725.
Mary, wife of John Baverick,
Hannah Haskell.

1726.
Desire Chaddick,
Philip Bemus,
Mercy Bemus.

1727.
Josiah Robbins,
Joseph English, Indian servant, living with William Russell,
Sarah Fowl,
Eunice Parks,
Richard Falley,
Henry Johnson,
Deborah Baverick,
Richard Muzaphen.

1728.
Pompey, a negro servant.

1729.
Rose, negro servant of A. Bordman.

1730.
John Morse,
Elizabeth Beard.

1731.
Sarah Wheatley.

1735.
Ruth, wife of Mathew Mallit.

1736.
Hannibal, servant of Dr. Wigglesworth,
Mary Welch,
Margaret, servant of the Widow Oliver.

1737.
Anna Joiner, daughter of Jonathan Baverick.

1739.
Roger, negro servant of Henry Prentice,
Zillah, negro servant of Major Brattle,
Ruth Cheney,
Mary Steel.

1740.
Lucy, an Indian, servant of Mr. Bordman,
Venus, negro servant of Madam Wadsworth,
Cuffy, negro servant of Lieut. Gov. Phipps,
Toby, servant of Samuel Whitemore,
Anna Elliset.

1741.
Jack, negro servant of Widow Tufts,
Cuffy, servant of Judah Monis,

Flora, negro servant of Mr. Foxcroft.

1742.
Anna Greenleaf,
York, a negro servant of Mr. Trowbridge,
Judith Cox.

1744.
Harry, a negro servant of Mr. Brandon,
Elizabeth Welch,
Hannah Welch.

1745.
Rose, negro servant of Lieut. Gov. Phipps,
Benjamin Cheney,
Cato, negro servant of Madam Brown.

1749.
Leos, negro servant of Mr. Foxcroft.

1753.
Jane, negro woman of Mr. Kent, the wife of Hannibal,
Jonathan Brooks.

1755.
James, negro servant of Lieut. Gov. Phipps,
Hannah Edmunds.

1760.
Peter, negro servant of Moses Bordman's widow,
Lydia, daughter of Dr. Francis Moores.

1761.
Cato, negro servant of Jonathan Hastings.

1762.
Joshua Thomas.

1763.
Mary Hephen,
Ensigne Man, a college student,
Tamazen Hastings.

1764.
Rebekah Kenney,
Samuel Hill.

1765.
Abigail Remick.

1768.
Jane, negro servant of Elizabeth Nutting.

1769.
Philip, negro servant of Abraham Watson.

1770.
Mary Lamb.

1771.
Jerusha, a negro woman living with Lieut. John Dickson,
Anne, negro servant of Jonathan Hastings, Esq.

1772.
Silas Robbins,
Lydia, wife of John Phillips.

1773.
Abigail Tufts.

1774.
Mary Blackman,
Mary Todd,
Anna, wife of George Douglass.

1775.
Thankfull, wife of Stephen Palmer, Jun.

1776.
Dilla, negro woman belonging to Samuel White.

1781.
Deborah Dickson.

1782.
Nathaniel Bowman.

MEMBERS IN FULL COMMUNION.

[The following List contains the names of the Members of the Church from its formation, as far as they are known. As there are no complete Church Records earlier than 1696, the List before that time is necessarily imperfect.]

Rev. Thomas Shepard, Pastor. February, 1636.

1636.

Thomas Shepard,
Mrs. Margaret Shepard,
John Haynes,
Mrs. Mabel H. Haynes,
" Elizabeth Green,
Guy Banbridge,
Mrs. Justice Banbridge,
John Bridge,
Edward Winship,
Mrs. Jane Winship,
" Elizabeth Winship,
Samuel Green,
Mrs. Jane Green,
" Sarah Green,
Roger Harlakenden,
Mrs. Elizabeth Harlakenden,
Joseph Cooke,
Mrs. Elizabeth Cooke,
George Cooke,
Mrs. Alice Cooke,
Nicholas Danforth,
Thomas Marriot,
Mrs. Susanna Marriot,
Samuel Shepard,
Mrs. Hannah Shepard,
William French,
Mrs. Elizabeth French,
Simon Crosby,
Mrs. Ann Crosby,
Thomas Cheescholme,
Mrs. Isabel Cheescholme,
John Russell,
Percival Green,
Mrs. Ellen Green,
Thomas Blodgett,
Mrs. Susan Blodgett,
Edmund Frost,
Mrs. Thomasine Frost,
" Mary Frost,
Thomas Judd,
Mrs. Thomas Judd,
Edward Goffe,
Mrs. Joyce Goffe,
" Margaret Goffe,
Richard Champney,
Mrs. Jane Champney,
Gregory Stone,
Mrs. Lydia Stone,
Gilbert Crackbone,
Mrs. Elizabeth Crackbone,
Thomas Beale,
Mrs. Sarah Beale,
Richard Parke,
Mrs. Sarah Parke,
William Clements,
Mrs. Martha Clements,
" Ann Clements.

1637.

Thomas Parish,
Mrs. Mary Parish,
Thomas Brigham,
Mrs. Mary Brigham,
William Cutter,
William Towne,
Mrs. Martha Towne,
John Gibson,
Mrs. Rebecca Gibson,
" Joane Ames,
" Joanna H. Shepard.

1638.

Michael Spencer,
Mrs. Rebecca Spencer,
Thomas Foxe,
John Sill,
Mrs. Joanna Sill,
George Willis,
Mrs. Jane Willis,
Thomas Swetman,
Mrs. Isabell Swetman,
Edward Hall,
Mrs. Margaret Hall,
Nathaniell Eaton,
Mrs. Nathaniell Eaton.

1639.

Roger Shawe,
Mrs. Ann Shawe,
Robert Daniel,
Mrs. Elizabeth Daniel,
" Reana Daniel,
Hezekiah Usher,
Mrs. Frances Usher,
" Elizabeth Usher,
" Mary Usher,
Christopher Cane,
Mrs. Margery Cane,
Robert Stedman,
Mrs. Anne Stedman,
Nathaniel Sparrowhawke,
Mrs. Mary Sparrowhawke,
" Katharine Sparrowhawke,
Robert Saunders.

1640.

William Andrews,
Mrs. Mary Andrews,
" Abigail Andrews,
John Stedman,
Mrs. Alice Stedman,
Edmund Angier,
Mrs. Ruth Angier,
Richard Francis,
Mrs. Alse Francis,
John Trumbull,
Mrs. Elizabeth Trumbull,
William Manning,
Mrs. Susanna Manning,
Edward Collins,
Mrs. Martha Collins.

1641.

Henry Dunster,
Mrs. Elizabeth Dunster,
" Elizabeth Dunster,
Robert Holmes,
Mrs. Jane Holmes,
Goldin Moore,
Mrs. Joane Moore,
Richard Cutter,
Mrs. Elizabeth Cutter,
John Fessenden,
Mrs. Jane Fessenden.

1642.

Edward Oakes,
Thomas Oakes,
Mrs. Elizabeth Oakes,
Roger Bancroft,

Mrs. Elizabeth Bancroft,
Richard Eckles,
Mrs. Mary Eckles,
John Cooper,
Mrs. Anna Cooper,
William Dickson,
Mrs. Jean Dickson.

1643.

John Knight,
John Jackson,
Mrs. John Jackson,
" Margaret Jackson,
Daniel Stone,
Mrs. Mary Stone,
Thomas Danforth,
Mrs. Mary Danforth,
Andrew Stephenson,
Mrs. Jane Stephenson,
William Manning,
Mrs. Dorothy Manning.

1644.

Daniel Gookin,
Mrs. Mary Gookin.

1645.

Herbert Pelham,
John Watson,
Mrs. Rebecca Watson,
Vincent Druse,
Mrs. Vincent Druse,
Nathaniel Green,
Mrs. Joanna Green,
Francis Griswold,
Mrs. Mary Griswold,
William Patten,
Mrs. Mary Patten,
Elijah Corlet,
Mrs. Barbara Corlet,
Edward Jackson,
Mrs. Frances Jackson,
" Elizabeth Jackson.

1646.

Matthew Day.

1647.

David Fiske,
Mrs. Lydia Fiske,
" Seaborne Fiske,
David Stone,
Mrs. Dorcas Stone,
Philip Cooke,
Mrs. Mary Cooke,
William Ames,
Daniel Kempster,
Mrs. Abigail Kempster,
Samuel Danforth,
Mrs. Mary Danforth,
Jonas Clark,
Mrs. Sarah Clark,
" Elizabeth Clark,
" Elizabeth Clark,
Samuel Hides,
Mrs. Temperance Hides,
" Elizabeth Luxford,
John Stansby,
Katharine (Mrs. Ruggles' mayd),
Bro. Jackson's mayd,
Hannah Brown,
John Furnell,
Mrs. Mary Furnell,
Edward Mitchenson,
Mrs. Ruth Mitchenson.

1650.

John Shepard,
Mrs. John Shepard,
James Prentice,
Mrs. Susanna Prentice,
Henry Prentice,
Mrs. Joane Prentice,

Rev. Jonathan Mitchell, Pastor. August 21, 1650.

Jonathan Mitchell,
Mrs. Margaret S. Mitchell.

1651.

Richard Oldham,
Mrs. Martha Oldham.

1652.

Francis Moore,
Mrs. Katharine Moore,
" Elizabeth Moore,
Daniel Blodgett,
Mrs. Mary Blodgett,
William Bordman,
Mrs. Frances Bordman.

1654.

Francis Whitmore,
Mrs. Isabell Whitmore,
John Green,
Mrs. Ruth Green,
Joseph Champney.

1656.

John Hasting,
Mrs. Anne Hasting,
Thomas Shepard,
Charles Chauncy,
Mrs. Catharine Chauncy.

1657.

Justinian Holden,
Mrs. Elizabeth Holden,
Samuel Stone,
Mrs. Sarah Stone.

1658.

Esther Sparrowhawke,
John Stone,
Elizabeth Stone,
Sarah Stone,
Lydia Fiske,
Barnabas Lampson,
Mrs. Dorcas Bridge,
Hannah Marriot,
Samuel Andrews,
Mrs. Elizabeth Andrews,
Edward Shepard,
Mrs. Violet Shepard,
" Mary Shepard,
Mrs. Olbon,
Andrew Belcher,
Mrs. Elizabeth Belcher,
John Palfrey.

1659.

Mary Towne,
Rebecca Stevenson,
James Kiddar,
Mrs. Anne Kiddar,
Ephraim Kiddar,
Walter Hasting,
Mrs. Sarah Hasting,
" Elizabeth Hasting,
William Hamlet,
Mrs. Sarah Hamlet,
Thomas Hubbard,
Mrs. Anne Errington,
Richard Daniel,
Mrs. Anne Daniel,
" Mary Paddlefoot,
" Sarah Barret.

1661.

Mrs. Mary Barret,
Stephen Day,
Mrs. Mary Goave,
" Hannah Goffe,

Mrs. Frances Embsden,
Samuel Champney,
Sarah Champney.

1663.

Lydia Champney,
David Champney,
Samuel Shepard,
Elizabeth Stedman,
Francis Moore,
Mrs. Abby Moore,
Nicholas Wyeth,
Mrs. Rebecca Wyeth,
William Heily,
Mrs. Grace Heily,
" Phebe Heily,
Hannah Heily,
Abraham Errington,
Mrs. Rebeckah Errington,
" Mary Mitchenson,
James Hubbard,
Mrs. Deborah Makoon,
Thomas Prentice,
Mrs. Grace Prentice,
Jonathan Hyde,
Mrs. Mary Hyde,
Zechariah Hicks,
Mrs. Elizabeth Hicks,
Abraham Holman,
Mrs. Holman.

1664.

Mrs. Samuel Collins,
John Whyting,
Mrs. Sybill Whyting,
Sarah Stedman,
Thomas Parke,
Mrs. Abigail Parke,
James Prentice,
Mrs. Susanna Prentice,
Nathaniel Sparrowhawke,
Mrs. Patience Sparrowhawke,
Martha Stedman,
Richard Jackson,
Mrs. Elizabeth Jackson,
" Mary Russell.

1665.

Stephen Willowes,
John Marriot,
Mrs. Abigail Marriot,
George Cooke,
James Trowbridge,
Mrs. Margaret Trowbridge,
" Margaret Trowbridge,
John Grout,
Mrs. Mary Grout,
" Sarah Grout,
Joseph Easterbrooke,
Mrs. Mary Easterbrooke,
Mary Gookin,
Elizabeth Gookin,
John Holmes,
Mrs. Seeth Rosse,
" Mary Hancock.

1666.

Joseph Cook,
Edward Collins,
Mrs. Martha Collins,
John Collins,
Martha Belcher,
Mrs. Anne Bridge,
" Sarah Longhorn,
Richard Robbins,
Mrs. Rebecca Robbins,
Hannah Moore,
William Bullard,
Mrs. Mary Bullard,
Mr. Wells,
Mrs. Bethiah Wells,
Elizabeth Swetman,

John Taylor,
Mrs. Katharine Taylor,
Robert Parker,
Mrs. Robert Parker,
Benjamin Parker,
John Parker,
Sarah Parker,
Rachel Parker,
Thomas Brown,
Mrs. Esther Cheever,
Solomon Prentice,
Abiah Prentice,
Samuel Prentice,
Sarah Prentice,
Henry Prentice,
Mrs. Deborah Wilson,
Richard Hassell,
Mrs. Joane Hassell,
Thomas Prentice,
Mrs. Grace Prentice,
" Mary Hall,
John Adams,
Mrs. Anne Adams,
Mrs. Elizabeth Hall,
Robert Browne,
John French,
Mrs. Joanna French,
Sarah French,
Mrs. Jeremiah Sill,
Thomas Fillebrowne.

1669.

Nathaniel Hancock,
Mrs. Hannah Holmes,
" Martha Russell.

Rev. Urian Oakes, Pastor. November 8, 1671.

1671.

Urian Oakes.

Rev. Nathaniel Gookin, Pastor. November 15, 1682.

1682.

Nathaniel Gookin,
Mrs. Nathaniel Gookin.

Rev. William Brattle, Pastor. November 25, 1696.

1696.

William Brattle,
Mrs. William Brattle,
Thomas Danforth,
Mr. Andrews,
Samuel Kidder,
Samuel Cooper,
Nathaniel Hancock and wife,
Andrew Bordman,
Ruth Bordman,
Wife of Edward Marriot,
Samuel Manning,
Joseph Hicks,
Isaac Knap,
Sr. Blower,
Thomas Symms,
Goody Luxford,
Bethiah Hicks,
Deborah Squire,
Hannah Chandler,
Mary Green,
Daniel Cheever,
Jacob Dana,
Joseph Winship and wife,
Wife of Nathaniel Patten,
" Philip Goodwin,

Wife of Joseph Champney,
Elizabeth Blower,
Elizabeth Collis,
Daniel Dana and wife,
Wife of Thomas Stacy,
Stephen Palmer and wife,
Wife of John Wyeth,
" John Bunker,
John Stedman and wife.

1697.

Nathaniel Saltonstall,
Anthony Stoddard, Jun.,
Jabez Wakeman,
Jonathan Green,
Wife of Edmund Goffe,
Widow Batson, *alias* Goody Walden,
Widow Hill,
Wife of Samuel Manning,
" Ebenezer Brown,
" Elisha Bull,
Lydia Pratt,
Mrs. Martha Remington,
Hannah Hamlett,
Mr. Fitch,
David Deming, Senior, and wife,
Jacob Amsdall and wife,
Zechariah Hicks, Jun., and wife,
Wife of Robin Webber,
" Jonathan Pierce,
" Solomon Prentice, Jun.,
John Bonner,
John Collis,
Daniel Woodward and wife,
Wife of William Barrett,
Hannah Goodwin,
Benjamin Dana,
John Manning and wife,
Mrs. Homer,
Sarah Gilly.

1698.

Nicholas Fessenden, Senior,
Solomon Hancock,
Wife of Dr. Oliver,
Elizabeth Brattle,
Wife of Samuel Cook,
Phebe Goffe,
William Russell and wife,
John Dickson and wife,
Jason Russell and wife,
Abraham Watson and wife,
John Brooker,
Widow Whiting,
Wife of John Cooper,
" Gershom Swan,
" Philip Cook,
Mary Oldham,
Nicholas Fessenden, Jun.,
Lydia Smith,
Rebeccah Andrews,
Elizabeth Robbins,
Mary Allin,
Wife of Ephraim Frost,
" Thomas Fillebrown,
" Joseph Adams,
" John Smith,
Rebeccah Palfrey,
Mary Batson.

1699.

Wife of John Oldham,
" Jacob Chamberlin,
" Ephraim Osborn,
Hannah Oldham,
Widow of Barnabas Cook,
Elizabeth Patten,
Percival Hall and wife,
Wife of Andrew Bordman.

1700.

Doctor Oliver,

Benjamin Goddard,
Samuel Champney,
William Cutter and wife,
John Patten and wife,
Wife of Samuel Cooper,
Joseph Crackbone and wife,
Hannah Hasting,
Sarah Lewis, Jun.,
Sr. Whiting,
Theophilus Cotton.

1701.

Sr. Elliot,
Hannah, the wife of Samuel Champney,
Sr. Angier,
Thomas Prentice,
Deborah Streeter, Senior,
Hannah, wife of Thomas Davis,
Lydia Francis,
Mary Marriot,
Samuel Ruggles,
Sarah, wife of Abraham Hill,
Mary, wife of Walter Russell,
Ruth Baverick.

1702.

Mr. Remington,
John Oldham,
Widow Gath,
Mr. Burr,
John Hall,
Jemimah Hall,
William Warland,
Tabitha Warland,
Ann Oldham,
Moses Bordman,
Abigail Bordman,
Nathaniel Robbins,
Elizabeth Cookworthy,
Dorothy Manning.

1703.

Daniel Hasting,
Abigail Hasting,
John Bradish,
Elizabeth Preston,
Robert Breck,
Joseph Coolidge and wife,
John Robbins,
Wife of Samuel Phipps,
Elizabeth Phipps,
Captain Parker and wife,
David Deming, student,
Wife of Jacob Watson,
Joseph Kent and wife,
Joseph Marsh, student,
Samuel Robinson,
Sarah Manning,
Ebenezer Swan and wife,
Goodwife Lewis,
Abigail Oldham,
Sr. Stoddard,
William Williams.

1704.

Goodman Squire,
" Clark,
" Davis,
" Smith,
Nathaniel Pierce and wife,
Wife of John Blower,
" John Knight,
Mrs. Lucy Bradstreet,
Mrs. Mary Hayman,
Hannah Needham,
Elizabeth Hicks,
Mehetabel Gale,
John Bradshaw,
Anna Collis,
Ruth Bradish,
Deborah Wyeth,
Mr. Goffe, Senior,

Jonathan Butterfield and wife,
Wife of James Clark,
Elizabeth Dana.

1705.

Peter Town,
Elizabeth Town,
Widow Coolidge,
Wife of Nathaniel Patten, Jun.,
Nathaniel Cutter and wife,
Ruth, wife of James Tuft,
Thomas Andrew,
Jonathan Peirce,
Thomas Prince, student,
John Gove, "
Stephen Hall, *i. e.* Stow Hall,
Grace, wife of Stephen Hall,
Widow Mary Gidney,
Rebecca Squire,
Hephzibah, wife of John Bradish.

1706.

Owen Warland,
Sr. Gookin,
Joseph Sewall,
Francis Whittemore and wife,
Stephen Frost and wife,
Ephraim Osborn,
Amos Gates,
Ebenezer Thayer, student,
David Jeffries, "
John Tufts, "
Eleazar Williams, "
John Webb, "
Mary Prentice,
John Swan, *exc.* and restored.

1707.

Benjamin Prescott, student,
Mrs. Priscilla Hayman,
Wife of Jonathan Gove,
Wife of Bartholomew Barrett,
John Cooper,
Sarah, wife of John Fessenden,
Widow Cheever,
Wife of Gershom Cutter, Jun.,
Mrs. Sybil Avery.

1708.

Ebenezer Brooks and wife,
Margaret Hicks,
Mrs. Mercy Bradstreet,
" Deborah Jackson,
Hannah, wife of Andrew Wilson,
Elizabeth, wife of J. Harrington,
Wife of Zechariah Heard.

1709.

Samuel Gookin and wife,
Nathaniel Sparrowhawke and wife,
Wife of Stephen Hasting,
Jonathan Hasting and wife,
Margaret Gates,
Mrs. Greenleaf,
Wife of Ebenezer Hancock,
" John Hill,
Experience Dana.

1710.

John Coit, student,
John Cutter and wife,
Wife of Joseph Crackbone,
Mr. Holyoke, student,
Thomas Livermore and wife,
Henry Dunster and wife,
Solomon Prentice,
Thomas Hall and wife,
Elisha Williams, student,
John Chipman, "
John Whittemore and wife.

1711.

Elisha Bull,
Nathaniel Patten,
John Fillebrown and wife,
Aaron Cleveland,
Sarah Biscoe,
John Williams and wife,
Samuel Brooks and wife,
Jonathan Hall and wife,
Stephen Williams, student,
Benjamin Crocker, "

1712.

Sarah Patten,
John Parker and wife,
Thomas Grover and wife,
Thomas Sewall,
Sr. Denison,
Sr. Appleton,
Thomas Foxcroft,
Susanna Winship,
Joanna Winship,
Sarah Cookesey.

1713.

Francis Foxcroft,
Sr. Rogers, student
Joseph Stacy,
Sr. Job Cushing student.

1714.

William Brown,
Edward Thwing,
Samuel Whittemore,
Joseph Cook,
Samuel Stow, student,
Eunice Cook,
Susanna Clark,
Goodman Webber,
Sarah, wife of J. Winship,
Susanna, wife of S. Gookin,
Anne Parker,
Prudence Hancock,
Samuel Terry, student,
Sr. Berry, "
John Gardner, "
Samuel Spear, "
Benjamin Webb, "
James Read and wife,
Stephen Prentice and wife,
Nathanael Prentice and wife,
John Foord,
Mrs. Samuel Sparrowhawke,
Abiel Hovey,
Goody Burgess, Senior,
Elizabeth Berry,
Mercy Oliver,
Mercy Chapman,
Margaret Hicks.

1715.

John Lawrence and wife,
Wife of Daniel Squire,
William Fessenden,
Margaret Fessenden,
Josiah Bond,
John Hicks,
Sarah Agar,
Rebeccah Coolidge,
Ruth Hicks.

1716.

George Abbot and wife,
Nathaniel Cotton,
Francis Kidder,
John Manning,
Elizabeth Smith,
Wife of Jonathan Gates,
" Isaac Watson,
Sarah Kidder,
Elizabeth Stacy,
Ruth Bordman,

Col. Phipps,
Hezekiah Gould,
Elizabeth Bordman,
Elizabeth Gardner,
Sr. Brown,
Joseph Moodey,
Deborah Gammage,
Martha Wyeth,
Nathaniel Robbins, Jun.,
Wife of Samuel Angier,
" Nathaniel Robbins,
Sir Cheekley,
Elkanah Osborn,
Samuel Scott,
Joseph Adams,
Thomas Frost,
Thomas Fillebrown, Jun.,
Rebecca Ingham,
Sarah Scott,
Elizabeth, wife of Walter Russell,
Elizabeth, wife of Holmit Russell,
Mary Frost,
Sarah Frost,
Mary Frazier.

1717.

Warham Williams, student,
Solomon Williams, "
Samuel Dana,
Ebenezer Fessenden,
Samuel Prentice,
John Knight,
Elizabeth Nutting,
Martha Moore,
Mary Dana.

Rev. Nathaniel Appleton, D. D., Pastor. October 9, 1717.

Nathaniel Appleton,
Dorothy Manning,
Ephraim Frost,
John Hancock, student,
Bethiah Champney,
Samuel Andrews,
Nathaniel Oliver and wife,
Gershom Davis and wife,
William Winship and wife,
Nathaniel Leonard, student,
Wife of Nathaniel Cutter,
" Nathaniel Winship,
" Francis Kidder,
Elizabeth Andrews.

1719.

Jacob Watson,
Joseph Robbins and wife,
Abigail Hancock,
Margery Dickson,
Samuel Angier,
Samuel Felch,
Katharine Felch,
William Rand, student,
Mary Langley,
John Cook,
Jonathan Butterfield,
Esther Cheever,
William Manning,
Consider Lycore,
Tabitha Hancock.

1720.

Mrs. Margaret Appleton,
William Cook,
Benjamin Balch,
John Cooper,
Nimphus Stacy,
Susannah Dana,
Eleaner Phipps,

Elizabeth Prentice,
Nathaniel Tufts,
Thomas Clapp, student,
Mrs. Sarah Leverett,
" Mary Denison,
Mary, wife of Thomas Dana,
Nathaniel Rogers, student,
Jonathan Nutting, Jun.,
Rachel Stone,
Alice, wife of James Cutter,
Mary Hicks,
Jonathan Gove,
Mary Champney,
Rebecca Champney,
Sr. Eliot,
Dorothy, wife of James Upham,
William Dickson and wife,
Thomas Kidder,
Widow Elizabeth Pierce.

1721.

Huldah Russell,
Margery Winship,
Abigail Butterfield,
Elizabeth Sangor,
Gershom Cutter, Senior,
Daniel Champney,
Walter Cooper,
Mary Cooper,
Martha Goddard.

1722.

Sr. Cotton, student,
John Tuck, "
David Hall, "
Josiah Smith,
Joseph Russell,
Sr. Hunting,
Henry Prentice,
Elizabeth Prentice,
Mary, wife Abraham Hill, Jun.,
John Warren, student,
Samuel Bowman,
Mary Bowman,
Edward Manning and wife,
John Comer.

1723.

John Sturgis, student,
Abraham Watson,
Eunice Angier,
Peter Hurd,
Mary Robbins,
Nathan Basset,
Samuel Cutter and wife,
Edward Hunting, student,
Elizabeth Cooper,
Elizabeth Prentice,
Edmund Frost and wife,
John Swan,
Joseph Crackbone,
Wife of Joseph Winship, Jun.,
Mary, wife of Ebenezer Burgess,
Sr. Hancock,
Samuel Holding,
Samuel Cooper,
William Cutter and wife,
Thomas Robbins,
Mary, wife of William Manning,
Elizabeth Hancock.

1724.

Susannah, wife of Samuel Holding,
Priscilla Dana,
Francis Lock and wife,
Abraham Hill, Jun.,
Widow Lydia Cooper,
Noah Champney,
Mary, wife of Nathaniel Tufts,
William Osgood,
Joseph Champney,
Hepzibah, wife of John Robbins
Hannah Cutter.

1725.

John Williams, student,
Sir White, "
Thomas Prentice, "
Joseph Kent, Jun.,
Anne, wife of William Cutter,
Anna Fillebrown,
Mary, wife of Joseph Shed,
Benjamin Kent, student,
Zachary Hicks, "
Ebenezer Frost and wife,
Solomon Prentice, student,
Joseph Lord, "
Stephen Kent,
Samuel Rand,
Jacob Hill,
John Winship and wife,
William Barrett, Jun.,
Abigail, wife of Mr. Monis,
Mary, wife of John Prentice,
Elizabeth Barrett.

1726.

Stephen Sewall,
William Brattle,
James Chandler, student,
John Dickson, Jun.,
Ebenezer Wyeth and wife,
Sarah, wife of Andrew Willson,
Margaret Patten,
Sarah Fessenden,
Elizabeth Fessenden,
Edward Barrett.

1727.

Samuel Danforth,
Stephen Palmer and wife,
Sarah, wife of Samuel Smith,
Mary, wife John Dickson, Jun.,
Sir Rogers, Senior,
Samuel Sparrowhawke,
John Burgess,
Martha Brown,
Abigail Brown,
Anna Fillebrown,
Mary Kidder,
Hannah Kidder,
Joanna, wife of Samuel Cook, Jun.,
Caleb Dana and wife,
Samuel Belcher and wife,
Jonathan Belcher, student,
Sir Cutter, "
Joseph Fish, "
Joseph Manning, "
Nathan Mayhew, "
Ichabod Brown,
Joseph Winship,
John Wyeth,
Ephraim Osborn,
Downing Champney,
Richard Champney,
Benjamin Edey,
Margaret, wife of Isaac Manning,
Elizabeth, wife of Philip Bemus,
Elizabeth Hoar,
Exena Jackson,
Sarah Osborn,
Mary Coolidge,
Martha Dunster,
Mehetabel Cutter,
Matthew Abdy,
Ruth Abdy,
Stephen Coolidge,
Sir Rogers, Jun.,
Joshua Gammage,
Thomas Robbins,
Nathaniel Eells, student,
David Stearns, "
Philemon Robbins, "
Joseph Mayhew, "
Thomas Tyler, "

1728.

William Williams, student,
Sir Stedman, "
Enoch Freeman, "
Perley Howe, "
John Wood, "
Henry Prentice, Jun.,
Christopher Bridge,
Hannah, wife of Eleazer Parker,
Sarah Nutting,
Mary Nutting,
Lydia Champney,
Ruth Champney,
Susannah Champney,
Mary Swan,
Lydia Cutter,
Martha Russell,
Bethiah Grover,
Edward Dickson,
John Kidder,
Nathaniel Kidder,
Benjamin Goddard, Jun.,
Sarah, wife of Edward Russell,
Deborah Cressen,
Nicholas Bows,
Daniel Champney, Jun.,
James Jackson,
Phinehas Hemmenway, student,
Jonathan Hastings, "
Sarah, wife of Ephraim Frost.

1729.

Benjamin Vial, student,
James Diamond, "
Hannah, wife of Thomas Soden,
Jane Hubbard,
Thomas Champney,
Priscilla, wife of Nathaniel Sparrowhawke,
Titus, Indian servant of Pres. Wadsworth,
Elizabeth, wife of John Robbins,
John Gove,
Lydia Gove,
Mary Gove,
Luxford Patten and wife,
Jonathan Cooper,
Rebecca Cutter,
Lydia Cutter,
Mary Dunster,
Abigail Dunster.

1730.

Thomas Hall and wife,
Thomas Sparrowhawke,
Mrs. Martha Bridge,
Josiah Robbins,
James Bradish,
Ruth Butterfield,
Jane, wife of George Cutter,
Dorothy Angier,
Ephraim Avery, student,
Henry Gibbs, "
John Prentice, Jun.,
Elizabeth Bordman,
Deborah Robbins,
Samuel Prentice,
Abigail Bordman.

1731.

Thomas Williams,
Walter Russell, Jun.,
Mary, wife of Solomon Hancock,
Abigail, wife of Ebenezer Shed,
Mary, wife of James Osborn,
Philicia, servant of Maj. Brattle,
Phœbe Patten,
Phœbe Butterfield,
Mary, wife of Thomas Sparrowhawke,
Joseph Been and wife,
Peter Tufts,

Ebenezer Shed,
Mrs. Lucy Remington,
" Martha Remington,
Elizabeth Bradish.

1732.

Ebenezer Cutter and wife,
Thomas Goddard,
Martha Hancock,
Lydia Mores,
Jemima, the wife of Jonathan Baverick,
Hannah Cook,
Elizabeth Cook,
James Peirce,
Deborah Brown,
Hannah Cutter.

1733.

Mehetabel Kent,
Deborah Baverick,
Edward Marriot,
Sir Sparrowhawke, student,
" Breck, "
" Porter, "
" Winthrop, "
Thomas Balch, "
Hannah Angier,
Elisabeth Whittemore,
Sarah Robbins,
Mary, wife of Samuel Hopkins,
Amos Marriot, Jun.,
Hannah Frost,
Elizabeth Frost,
Jonathan Edmunds,
Widow Mary Oliver,
Sarah, wife of Jacob Hill, Jun.

1734.

Walter Hastings,
Jeremiah Russell,
Samuel Kent,
Joanna, wife of Deacon Samuel Sparrowhawke,
Sarah Hill,
Caleb Rice,
Sarah, wife of Thomas Williams,
Deborah Bowman,
John Cutter,
Mary Fessenden,
Mary Brown,
Rebecca Dill.

1735.

Mary Balch,
Ebenezer Prentice and wife,
Enoch Ward, student,
Sir Cook, "
Joshua Tufts "
Jonas Prentice,
Edmund Goffe, *alias* Trowbridge,
Sarah, wife of Josiah Robbins.

1736.

William Prentice,
Nathaniel Prentice,
James Perry,
Isaac Warren,
Thomas Barrett,
Thomas Soden,
Hannah Livermore,
Joshua Rand,
Timothy Harrington, student,
Francis Smith,
Jonathan Haywood,
Judah Monis,
Margaret, servant of the Widow Oliver.

1737.

Mrs. Mary Remington,
Lydia Warren,

Elisabeth Winship,
Jedidiah Adams,
Richard Pateshall, B. A.,
John Phillips, B. A.,
Ebenezer Gay, student,
Edmund Frost, Jun.,
Isaac Morse,
Mary, wife Edw. Marriot, Jun.,
Sarah Stratton,
Hezekiah Man,
Benjamin Brozier and wife,
Mary, wife of Daniel Hovey,
Mary Cutter,
John Goddard,
Martha, wife of Andrew Mallet,
Sophia, wife of —— Deeks,
Margaret Whittemore.

1738.

Sarah, wife of Jonathan Cooper,
Elizabeth Lock,
Lydia Bradfield,
Sir Eliot Andrew, student,
Nehemiah Cutter,
Mary, wife of Abraham Watson,
Sarah, wife of Joshua Rand,
Joseph Adams, Jun.,
Ephraim Frost,
Samuel Frost,
Martha Frost,
Abigail Cutter,
Mary Kidder,
Katharine, the wife of Richard Champney.

1739.

William Fessenden, Jun., B. A.,
Susannah Torrey,
Elizabeth Winship,
Edward Marriot, Jun.,
Jeremiah Wheelwright,
Daniel Prentice,
Sarah, wife of Moses Harrington,
Rebekah Adams,
Stephen Fessenden, B. A.,
Oxenbridge Thatcher, B. A.,
Matthew Cox,
Matthew Bridge, student,
Martha, wife of Nehemiah Cutter,
Martha Bordman,
Mary Bordman,
Stephen Prentice, Jun.,
Mercy, wife of Jonas Prentice.

1740.

Elizabeth, wife of Joseph Cook,
Sarah Hinde,
William Morse,
William Angier,
John Whittemore,
Ruth Whittemore,
Caleb Prentice,
Samuel Angier,
Jemima, wife Abraham Hossey,
Margaret Appleton,
Mary Stibbins,
Mary Man,
Jonathan Wyeth,
Joshua Prentice, B. A.,
James Read,
Sarah Wyeth,
Rebekah Morse,
Anna Morse,
Abigail Grant,
Prudence Hill,
Elizabeth Palmer.

1741.

Isaac Fillebrown and wife,
Joseph Cook,
William Warland,
Thomas Robbins, Jun.,

William Lawrence, student,
James Mills, student,
Elizabeth Livermore,
Anne Remington,
Lydia Whittemore,
Sarah Gammage,
Mary, daughter of Jacob Hill,
Lydia Shed,
Hannah Fillebrown,
Mercy Tufts,
Mary Hovey,
Margaret Ireland,
Mary, daughter of Abraham Hill,
Anne Elliston,
Mary Bafoot,
Hannibal, negro of Dr. Wigglesworth,
Roger, negro of Henry Prentice,
Rosa, negress of Mr. Bordman,
Joseph Been, Jun.,
Owen Warland,
Francis Winship,
Samuel Hastings,
Sarah Chadwick,
Thamazen Ireland,
Martha Prentice,
Abigail Hill,
Widow Lydia Pettis,
Sarah, wife of A. Bordman, Jun.,
Mary, wife of Thomas Ireland,
Hannah Smith, *alias* Daniels,
Abigail Bowman,
Susannah Soden,
Mary Parker,
Jonathan Ireland,
Samuel Bird, student,
Mehetabel Foxcroft,
Lydia Prentice,
Elizabeth Mallet,
Mary, wife Andrew Mallet, Jun.,
William Dana and wife.

1742.

Andrew Sever and wife,
Eliphalet Robbins and wife,
John Oldham,
Jemima Robbins,
Widow Mindwell Fessenden,
Elizabeth, wife of Matthew Cox,
Sarah Hastings,
Hannah Hastings,
Abigail Hastings,
Susannah Dana,
Samuel Cook,
Solomon Robbins,
Rebecca Hicks,
Mary Angier,
Nathaniel Gammage,
Elizabeth Appleton,
Elizabeth Foxcroft.

1743.

Andrew Bordman,
Benjamin Stevens,
Abigail, the wife of Solomon Champney,
Elizabeth, the wife of Jonathan Fessenden.

1744.

Matthew Cushing,
Abraham Hossey,
John Brown,
Martha Switcher,
Solomon Prentice, Jun.

1745.

Hannah, wife of Noah Bordman,

1746.

Lydia Kidder,
Sarah, wife of Abiel Richardson,
Gad Hitchcock,

1747.

Ebenezer Thompson,
Widow Lucy Vassall.

1748.

Oliver Peabody, B. A.,
Rebekah Wigglesworth,
Jonathan Read and wife,
Mary, wife of Samuel Hastings,
Naomi, wife of Ebenezer Frost, Jun.,
Mary Sanderson,
Stephen Palmer, Jun.,
Mehetabel Appleton,
Susannah Hastings.

1749.

John Dana and wife,
Sarah Rand,
Mary Winship,
Deborah, wife of Daniel Prentice,
Elizabeth Prentice,
Susannah Bowman.

1751.

John Ellis, Jun., B. A.,
Ebenezer Shed, Jun., and wife.

1752.

Nathan Tufts,
John Stratton and wife,
Abigail, wife Abiel Richardson,
John Rand, A. M.,
Jason Haven, student.

1753.

Jonathan Brooks,
John Hastings,
Abraham Cutting,
Moses Richardson,
Lydia Tufts,
Bethiah, wife of John Ellis,
Alice, wife Ebenezer Fessenden.

1754.

Capt. Ebenezer Stedman,
Mervial Brown,
Hepzibah Prentice,
Martha Hill,
Martha Sparrowhawke,
Elizabeth Holyoke,
Anna Holyoke,
Henry Coolidge and wife,
Mary Wigglesworth,
Jane, negress of Widow Kent,
Hannah, wife of James Read,
Dr. John Wright,
Anna, wife of Josiah Morse.

1755.

Mary, wife Henry Prentice, Jun.,
Florence, wife of —— Wyman
Elizabeth Dana,
Edward Thayer, B. A.,
Elias Smith, B. A.,
Peter Tufts, Jun.

1756.

William Gammage and wife,
James Frost and wife,
Tabitha, wife of William How,
Elizabeth Epes,
Priscilla Holyoke,
Sybill Sparrowhawke,
Lucy Sparrowhawke,
Rebekah Gammage,
Sarah Hill,
Jacob Watson and wife,
Isaac Watson,
Aaron Hill,
John Caldwell,
Tabitha Kidder.

1757.

Lydia, wife of Peter Tufts,
Mary Rand,
Anna, wife of William Rand,
Mary Thatcher,
Nathaniel Sparrowhawke and wife,
William Kneeland, tutor.

1758.

Samuel Locke, M. A.,
Elizabeth, wife of Samuel Sparrowhawke, Jun.,
Esther, wife of James Honeywell,
Sarah Sparrowhawke,
Dorothy Sparrowhawke.

1759.

Ebenezer Wyeth,
James Lovel, B. A.,
Anna, wife of Josiah Mason,
Thomas Gardner and wife,
Sarah Gardner,
Katherine Sparrowhawke,
Mary Larned.

1760.

Susannah, wife Samuel Choate,
Joshua Phipps and wife,
Abigail Gove.

1761.

Samuel Rand, Jun., and wife,
Amos Toppan, M. A.,
John Wyeth, B. A.

1762.

Amos Marriot and wife.

1763.

Abigail Prentice,
Ensign Man, student,
Elizabeth Wyeth,
Hannah Bowman,
Isaac Hossey, B. A.,
Hannah Haley,
Rachel Haley.

1764.

James Munroe and wife,
Christopher Marsh, B. A.,
Widow Hannah Sprague,
Eunice Kidder,
Rachel Kent,
Rebekah Rockwell,
Jonathan Crane, B. A.,
Phœbe Foxcroft,
Anna Dana.

1765.

Jonas Prentice, Jun.,
Widow Mercy Cooper,
Stephen Sewall,
Mary, wife of John Kidder.

1766.

Abraham Watson, Jr., and wife,
Joanna Cook,
Sarah Cook,
Mansfield Tapley and wife.

1767.

Sarah Stedman,
Lydia Moores,
Jane Boucher,
Esther, wife of James Bryne,
Sarah Watts,
Hannah Kidder,
Caleb Prentice, Jun., B. A.

1768.

Nathaniel Ward, B. A.,

Ebenezer Manning, B. A.,
Stephen Hall, B. A.,
Joseph Smith,
Margaret Fessenden,
Mary Burton,
Jonathan French, student,
Rebekah Kent.

1769.

Joseph Pierce Palmer, student,
Elizabeth Brandon,
Elizabeth Stedman,
Rachel Waters,
Sarah Bradish,
Susannah Foster,
Rebekah Oliver,
Stephen Peabody, student,
Prudence Wyeth,
Tabitha Champney,
Mary Hancock,
Sarah Hancock,
William Mayhew, B. A.,
James Miller, Jun.,
Violet, negress of Mr. Tuncuil.

1770.

Gideon Frost,
Isaac Mansfield, B. A.,
Thomas Miller,
Hannah, wife of Nathaniel Sparrowhawke,
Joseph Miller and wife,
Elizabeth Goddard,
Mary Dana,
Elizabeth Bond,
Timothy Tufts and wife,
Thomas Read,
Daniel Watson and wife,
Jonas Wyeth and wife,
Richard Honeywell and wife,
John Watson,
Mary, wife of John Nutting,
Sarah Read,
Henry Dickson,
John Walton and wife.

1771.

Samuel Smith Larned and wife,
Widow Elizabeth Champney,
Moses Adams, student,
Simeon Pratt and wife,
Charity Raymond,
Lucy Dana,
Mary Dickson,
Mary Phillips,
Seth Hastings and wife,
William Dana and wife,
Jonathan Cook and wife,
Widow Martha Prentice,
Mary Lamb,
Abigail Pratt,
Mary Mansfield,
Joanna Eames.

1772.

Benjamin Guild, B. A.,
Christiana Wainwright,
Betty, wife of Noah Wyeth,
Lois Fitch.

1773.

Aaron Tufts and wife,
Nathan Watson and wife,
Samuel Prentice, B. A.,
John Putnam,
Deborah, wife of Henry Collins,
Eunice Mansfield,
Josiah Temple and wife,
Mary, wife of Joshua Converse,
Jonathan Hastings, Jun., A. M.,
Nathaniel Jarvis and wife,
Eunice Bradish,

Elizabeth Cook,
Eunice Cook,
Abigail Moores,
Christiana, wife of —— Fuller,
Jemima Hossey.

1774.

Sarah Warland,
Theodore Parsons, B. A.,
Elizabeth Clough,
Edward Wigglesworth (Rev.), Hollis Professor at College,
Samuel Haven, B. A.,
Mary, wife of Stephen Greenleaf,
Martha Brandon,
Mary Pitts,
Samuel Fillebrown,
Mary Appleton,
Katherine Wendell,
Rebecca Hastings.

1775.

Rev. Dr. Samuel Langdon, President of College.

1776.

Martha Wright,
Benjamin Butterfield and wife.

1777.

Ruth, wife of James Jones,
Susannah Bowman,
Anna Shed,
Elizabeth Flucker,
James Freeman, B. A.

1778.

Jonathan Eames, B. A.,
Elisha Parmele, "

1779.

William Prentice, Jun.

1780.

Caleb Gannett (Rev.),
Widow Mary Durrant,
Thomas Hubbard Townsend.

1781.

Elizabeth, wife of Thomas Barrett,
Mary Kidder,
Thomas Marrett,
Stephen Goddard and wife,
Martha Fitch Wendell.

1782.

Katharine Morse,
Samuel Kendall, student,
Sarah, wife of Joseph Holden,
Beulah Prentice.

Rev. Timothy Hilliard, Pastor. October 27, 1783.

1783.

Timothy Hilliard,
Mary F. Hilliard (Timothy),
Rachel Crosbie,
Widow Bethiah Hackinson,
Mrs. Mary Mellen,
Mary Austin,
Walter Dickson and wife,
Anne Dickson.

1784.

Elizabeth Howe,
Tabitha Howe,
Amos Briant and wife.

1785.

Samuel Webber, A. B.,
Widow Eunice Walton,
Rebecca Hicks,
Martha Chapel,
Samuel Chandler.

1786.

Thomas Payson, A. B.,
Sarah Frost,
John Sawin and wife,
Mary, the wife of Thomas Payson, A. B.,
Benjamin Piper,
Henry Ware, A. B.

1787.

John Andrews, A. B.,
Widow Mary Stratton,
Mr. Thomas Lee,
William Harris, A. B.

1788.

Hezekiah Packard, A. B.,
Mrs. Mary Thacher.

1789.

James Winthrop, Esq.,
Thaddeus Mason Harris, A. B.,
Mrs. Elizabeth Hunt.

1790.

Polly Hilliard.

1791.

Pitt Clark.

Rev. Abiel Holmes, D. D., Pastor. January 25, 1792.

1792.

Abiel Holmes,
Mrs. Mary S. Holmes,
Sarah Pearson,
Elizabeth Bromfield,
Elizabeth Austin,
Bebe Moore,
Timothy Lindall Jennison,
Susan Thorn,
Jemima Flucker,
Catharine Morse.

1793.

Theodore Bliss,
Elizabeth Holyoke Kneeland,
Hannah Holden,
Sarah Manning,
Grace Child,
John Thornton Kirkland, tutor,
Mary Watson,
Hannah Morse,
Sarah Munro,
Walter Dickson, Jun., and his wife,
Lucy Dickson (Mrs. Sawin),
Mary Bates.

1794.

Elizabeth Stiles,
Nathaniel Prentiss,
Abigail Prentiss,
Lucy Stratten,
Sarah Rouse,
Rebecca Watson,
William Mason, resident graduate,
Joseph Hilliard.

1795.

Jonathan Whitaker, student,

Lucy Winship,
Aaron Learned.

1796.

Timothy Alden, res. gr.,
Nancy Seaver,
Sarah Bryant,
Luther Wright, res. gr.,
David Kendall, "

1797.

Catharine Gleason,
Huldah Bliss,
Andrew Bordman,
Freeman Parker, res. gr.

1798.

Levi Hedge, tutor,
Mary Tappan,
Nancy Bartlett,
Mary Bartlett,
Elizabeth Mason,
Mrs. Mehetable Hastings,
Sarah Goddard,
Isaac Allen, res. gr.,
Abraham Randall, res. gr.

1799.

Timothy Tufts, Jun.,
Submit Tufts,
Sidney Willard (Prof.),
Sophia Willard,
Mary Willard.

1800.

Lydia Kneeland,
Mary Kneeland,
Ann Mason,
Lucy Shed,
Patty Dickson,
Andrew Foster,
James Converse, res. gr.,
William Frothingham,
Joanna Dana,
Sarah Richards.

1801.

Mary Snow,
Elizabeth F. Prentiss,
Samuel Farrar, tutor,
Samuel Veazie, res. gr.,
John Dwight, res. gr.,
Persis Howard,
William Frost,
Lucy Frost.

1802.

William Ballard, res. gr.,
Jonas Wyeth, 3d,
Susan Wyeth,
Rebecca Rockwell,
Rebecca Webber,
Wm. Ellery Channing, Regent.

1803.

Rebecca Jarvis,
Susan Jarvis,
Abigail Jarvis,
William Dewey,
Mary Richardson,
John Stone,
Samuel Kent,
William Hilliard *(Deacon)*,
Mrs. Sarah L. Hilliard.

1804.

Maria Holyoke Pearson,
Margaret Bromfield Pearson,
Sarah Lee Bartlett,
Josiah Moore *(Deacon)*,
Nancy Moore,
Susan Prentiss,

Timothy Foster Rogers, res. gr.,
Sarah Fayerweather,
Mary Emilia Elizabeth Jennison,
Prof. Eliphalet Pearson, LL. D.

1805.

Charlotte Richardson,
Sarah Chadburne,
Isabella Hovey,
John Bartlett,
Galen Ware,
Katherine Brattle Gannett (Mrs. Bascom).

1806.

John Wilson Smith,
Catherine Walton,
James Munroe *(Deacon)*,
Mrs. Margaret Munroe (James),
Moses Webster, res. gr.

1807.

Amelia Tarbell,
Elizabeth Bowes,
Patty Trask.

1808.

James Foster,
Sophia Mellen,
Catharine Saltonstall Mellen,
Harriot Hilliard,
John Mellen (Rev.),
Susanna Morse,
Martha R. Dana (Mrs. Allston),
Elizabeth E. Dana,
Hannah Mason.

1809.

Prof. Henry Ware, D. D.,
Elizabeth Latham Gannett (Mrs Andrews),
Prof. John Farrar,
Deziah Barker Bell,
Mary Richardson,
Caroline Hastings.

1810.

Thomas Brattle Gannett (Rev.),
Elizabeth Wright,
Susanna Whitney.

1811.

Abel Whitney,
Samuel Sewall, A. M.,
Thomas Foster,
Samuel Bartlett,
Mary Bartlett,
Elizabeth Bartlett,
Susan Bartlett,
Joanna Bartlett,
John Dudley Andrews, res. gr.,
George B. English, res. gr.

1812.

Edward Everett, A. B., res. gr.,
Ruth Bradshaw (Mrs. Conant).

1813.

Simeon Putnam, A. B., res. gr.

1814.

Henry Ware, A. B.,
Lucy Ware,
Mary Ware,
Sarah Sessions,
Sophia Webber.

1815.

Ruth Blake,
Mary Munroe.

1816.

Esther Goodwin,
Sarah Flagg.

1817.

Deborah French,
Elizabeth Watson Waterhouse.

1818.

Whiting Cooley,
Mary Wesson,
Samuel F. Sawyer,
Mrs. Patience Sawyer (Samuel F.),
William Saunders,
Mrs. Sarah Saunders (William),
Mary Giddinge.

1819.

Nathaniel Munroe,
Torrey Hancock,
Isabella Hancock,
Ann Hunt,
Samuel Hunt.

1820.

Sarah Wesson,
Sarah Porter,
Elizabeth McDowell,
Ruth Jones Nelson.

1821.

William Bascom (Rev.),
Elizabeth Read.

1822.

Sarah Russell Barrett,
Mary Jackson Holmes,
Dinah Steed,
Samuel Manning, Jun.,
Mary Goddard,
Richard H. Dana.

1823.

Esther Read,
Mary Read,
Betsey Bates,
Elizabeth Holman,
Mrs. Rebecca Munroe (Nath'l).

1824.

Sylvanus Plympton,
Mary Bell Plympton,
Rosamond Putnam,
Susanna Gilson.

1825.

Mrs. Hannah Prentiss,
Sophia Willard Dana,
Ann Susan Holmes.

1826.

Amy E. McKeen (Mrs. J. E. Worcester),
Catharine Watson,
Sarah Lopeans,
Hannah Prentiss,
Elizabeth Watson,
Mary Smith,
Susan Holt.

1827.

Jesse Carter,
Catharine Smith,
Jonathan C. Prentiss,
Mrs. Mary Prentiss (Jona. C.),
Persis Bates,
Mrs. Lydia Parker,
Lydia Parker, 2d,

Mrs. Mary Thayer (Cephas P.),
Josiah W. Cook,
Marshall Tufts,
Sarah B. Coffin.

1828.

Sarah Ann Dana,
Abigail Dana,
Elizabeth Dana,
John Cragin,
Isabella J. Weeks,
Sarah Brown (Mrs. A. F. Shedd),
Mrs. Abigail Frost,
Jacob Potter,
Sarah Hancock (Mrs. J. W. Cook),
Hannah Read,
Elizabeth Hilliard.

1829.

Mrs. Sarah Anderson.

Rev. Abiel Holmes, D. D., Senior Pastor.

Rev. Nehemiah Adams, Junior Pastor. December 17, 1829.

Nehemiah Adams, Jun.,
Elizabeth Hilliard,
Thomas Dakin,
Eliza S. Newman.

1830.

Sophronia W. Houghton,
Mary Chadbourn,
Elizabeth Bates,
Mrs. Cynthia Russell (Thomas),
Mary Robbins (Mrs. James Hall),
Henry Nowell,
Mrs. Abigail Nowell (Henry),
David McClure,
Roxana Lane (Mrs. Cook),
Catherine Locke,
Mrs. Susan H. Bates (William, Senior),
Mrs. Abigail Gordon,
Elizabeth Palmer,
Mary Currier,
Susan F. Smith,
Louisa Sawyer (Mrs. Thurston),
Zoa Duntin (Mrs. Benjamin F. Wyeth),
Anna Bradshaw,
Martha Sawyer (Mrs. H. Lawrence),
Harriet Lowe,
Judith Lamson,
Calvin E. Stowe (Rev.),
Samuel Pickett,
Mrs. Nancy Pickett (Samuel),
Sarah Ann Wigglesworth (Mrs. Hobart),
Mary A. Sawyer (Mrs. Brower),
Caroline Hawkins (Mrs. E. K. Griffin),
Lucy Rice,
Elsey Kendall,
William Raymond.

1831.

Harriet C. Bowman,
Esther Symmes,
Lydia Norton,
Abigail J. Houghton,

Eunice Gilson (Mrs. Joseph Follett),
Huldah Knowlton,
Hannah Hawkins (Mrs. Griffin),
Hannah Read,
Joel Giles,
Alvah Cragin,
Alexander Lane,
Mrs. Mary Lerned (Thomas P.),
Mrs. Eliza Derby,
Mrs. Rowena Pratt (Dexter),
Martha Boardman,
Susan Chadman,
Miles Gardner,
Mrs. Lydia Gardner (Miles),
Hannah Barrett,
Margaret P. Washburn,
Mrs. Susan Cummings,
Philena Janes,
Susan Mears.

1832.

Martha W. Russell,
Thomas P. Lerned,
Emeline Brooks,
Mary Allen,
Aaron Pratt,
Enoch Noyes,
Charles Hayes,
Mrs. Martha H. Adams (Nehemiah),
Sarah Gates,
Stephen T. Farwell *(Deacon)*,
Mrs. Mary Stedman,
Anne Tolman (Mrs. D. N. Wright),
Charles Nowell,
Emeline Jones,
Miriam Gordon (Mrs. George Hayes),
Sarah Holt (Mrs. Nathaniel Mullikin),
Mrs. Sarah A. Little (Chas. C.).

1833.

Mrs. Rebecca Goodwin,
Emily Goodspeed,
Louisa Tolman (Mrs. Cate),
Rebecca Goodwin (Mrs. Charles Hayes),
Lucy Brown,
Sarah Goodwin.

1834.

Margaret Allen (Mrs. John Peacock),
Sarah Allen (Mrs. William Black),
Susan Allen (Mrs. James Munroe),
Mrs. Lucy Willard (Charles).

1835.

Mary S. Gould.

NOTE. Beginning with the year 1835, the letter *r* denotes admission by letter from another church; *t*, dismission to another church; *d*, deceased; *e*, excommunicated. Where there is no letter before the name the person was received upon confession of faith. There are a few surviving members whose date of admission was prior to the commencement of the references, beginning with the year 1808.

Rev. John A. Albro, D. D., Pastor. April 15, 1835.

April.	*r* John A. Albro, *d*
July.	*r* Mrs. Elizabeth S. Albro (John A.), *t*
September.	Nathaniel Mullikin, *t*
	r Mrs. Elizabeth C. Farwell (Stephen T.),
	r Mary Frost, *t*
	Theresa Gould (Mrs. Albert Stevens). *d*

1836.

January.	Caroline Wright (Mrs. Tufts), *t*
	Dorothea Derby (Mrs. Craig). *t*

1837.

January.	Sarah Joyce (Mrs. Thomas J. White),
	Hannah Little, *d*
	Eliza Gould, *d*
	Sarah E. Conant (Mrs. F. Nourse), *t*
	Hannah L. Conant (Mrs. Isaac A. Bassett), *t*
	r Mrs. Sarah H. Mullikin (Nathaniel), *t*
	Caroline Read (Mrs. Cragin), *t*
March.	Joseph Parker, *t*
	Mrs. Mary Parker (Joseph), *t*
May.	*r* Augustus D. Carpenter, *t*
	r Elsey Kendall (Mrs. T. P. Lerned), *d*
	Elizabeth Williams (Mrs. Clay). *t*

1838.

January.	*r* John Allen, *t*
March.	*r* William Greenough,
	r Mrs. Sarah Greenough (William),
May.	*r* Lyman Thurston,
	r Mrs. Delia Thurston (Lyman), *d*
	r Zelotes Hosmer, *t*
	r Mrs. Louisa Hosmer (Zelotes), *t*
	r Robert S. Rogers, *t*
	Mrs. Mary Ann Rogers (Robert S.), *t*
	r Benjamin A. Spaulding, *t*
	r David N. Wright, *d*
July.	Lucy D. Sawyer,
	Olive Abbott, *t*

November. Mary Frost, *t*
Susan Parker,
Eliza C. Parker.

1839.

January. *r* Alfred C. Carpenter, *t*
Francis Nourse, *t*
r Mrs. Mary Oliver, *t*
May. *r* Lyman Whiting, *t*
r Mrs. Sarah S. Hall (Orrin),
r Mrs. Hannah B. Priest, *d*
July. *r* Hannah Smith, *t*
September. *r* Elizabeth H. Rogers, *t*
November. Elizabeth Campbell (Mrs. Wilkinson), *t*
Anne Gould (Mrs. Albert Stevens),
Eliza J. Pike (Mrs. Fuller).

1840.

July. Mrs. Experience D. Hyde (Jonathan), *d*
Elizabeth L. Willard,
Harriet Lenard, *d*
Eunice Danforth, *t*
Clarissa Soule,
Henry Frost, *t*
Charles Lenox, *e*
September. Mrs. Lovey Dunham (Israel P.),
Louisa Gurney. *t*

1841.

September. *r* Benjamin A. Clarke,
r Mrs. Almira Clarke (Benjamin A.),
r Mrs. Harriet Walton (Nathan S.),
Delia A. Thurston,
November. *r* Sarah L. Clement (Mrs. Lyman Whipple). *t*

1842.

January. Ephraim S. Mullikin, *t*
Susannah Tufts, *t*
May. Jacob H. Bates, *d*
Charles Gould, *d*
William Bates, 2d, *d*

May. David W. Buck, *e*
William G. Dix, *t*
George Faulkner, *t*
David Campbell, *d*
Frederick A. Hunt, *e*
George S. Saunders,
Francis B. Washburn, *t*
Frederick A. Mumler,
Susan M. Green, *t*
Sarah Munroe,
Deborah P. Hodgden (Mrs. Fleming), *d*
Mary E. Pickett,
Sarah Brown, *t*
Lucy A. Divoll (Mrs. D. W. Buck), *d*
Nancy L. Divoll (Mrs. Cutting), *t*
Rowena Divoll (Mrs. William Bates, 2d), *d*
Sarah Lenard, *d*
Ann Maria Pickett (Mrs. Blanchard), *t*

September. *r* John Frazier, *d*
r Mrs. Elizabeth Frazier, *t*
r Milley Duntin, *d*
Lydia Hovey, *d*
Sarah Pike, *t*
Mary L. K. Conant (Mrs. Richard Streeter), *t*
Anne Reed, *d*
William Mills, *t*
Edward P. Chase, *t*

November. *r* Cynthia Dickson (Mrs. Isaac N. Stone), *t*

December. *r* Asa Gray,
r Amos Whittemore,
r Mrs. Almira Whittemore (Amos),
Charles Short. *t*

1843.

March. Josiah Chandler,

May. Mrs. Susan Harty, *d*

July. Mrs. Margaret Gibson (Mrs. G. Hartness),
Sarah Ross (Mrs. John Allen), *t*

September. *r* Frederick A. Frost, *t*
r Adeline Darling (Mrs. F. A. Frost), *t*
r Catharine Green (Mrs. Senter). *t*

1844.

March. *r* Otis Danforth, *t*
r Mrs. Selina Danforth, *t*
July. *r* Mrs. Harriette Blake Mills, *d*
r Charles Stratton,
r Mrs. Eunice Stratton (Charles).

1845.

March. Lucy C. Willard (Mrs. G. S. Saunders),
r Edmund Hayes,
r Mrs. Eliza Hayes (Edmund),
May. *r* William L. Ropes, *t*
Sarah Ropes,
William Sewall, *t*
Edward H. Ladd, *t*
September. *r* John Whipple,
r Mrs. Whipple (John),
r Lyman Whipple, *t*
Mrs. Louisa Whipple (Lyman). *d*

1846.

March. *r* Charles W. Homer *(Deacon)*,
r Mrs. Adeline D. Homer (Charles W.),
John S. Albro,
Sarah E. Albro, *t*
Charlotte A. Lyman,
r Mary Lyman,
r Catharine D. Lyman, *t*
r Hiram Sands, *t*
r Mrs. Sarah Sands (Hiram), *t*
r Annie Jean Lyman (Mrs. Charles Short), *t*
July. *r* Mrs. Lydia A. Kennard,
September. *r* Harriet Burrill (Mrs. Curtis Lawrence). *t*

1847.

January. Margaret McLaughlin, *t*
John McGee, *t*
Mrs. Margaret McGee, *t*
March. Eliza M. Judkins, *t*
July. Lewis H. Boutelle, *t*

July. *r* Adeline D. Homer (Mrs. W. G. Ladd, Jr.), *t*
September. *r* William G. Ladd, *t*
r Margaret C. Ladd, *t*
r William G. Ladd, Jr., *t*
Margaret C. Ladd (Mrs. Green), *t*
r Luther S. Hayes,
r Mrs. Emeline S. Hayes (Luther S.),
November. *r* Eben N. Horsford,
r Mrs. Mary G. Horsford (Eben N.), *d*
r William H. Hills, *d*
r Mrs. Elizabeth I. Hills (William H.), *t*
r Charles Demond, *t*
r Mary N. Clay (Mrs. Gates). *t*

1848.

January. *r* Mrs. Mary J. Gardiner,
r Lorana P. Delano,
r Mrs. Margaret Weatherston, *d*
r Margaret F. Weatherston, *t*
r Catharine Ramsay,
September. *r* John Benson, *d*
r Mrs. Lucy A. Benson (John), *d*
r Asa Bullard, *t*
r Mrs. Lucretia G. D. Bullard (Asa), *t*
r Charles S. Homer,
r Mrs. Henrietta M. Homer (Charles S.),
r Eliza Ann Wells,
r Josephine Kneeland, *t*
Charles W. Homer, Jr., *t*
Shattuck Hartwell, *t*
November. *r* Mrs. Mary Merrill.

1849.

January. *r* Isaac A. Bassett, *t*
Charles C. Little, *t*
July. Andrew Stewart, *d*
Mrs. Ellen Stewart (Andrew),
Samuel D. Hosmer, *t*
Isabella E. Kelsey, *t*
September. William A. Saunders,

September. Mrs. Mary P. Saunders (William A.),
r William A. Brewer, *t*
r Mrs. Marcy S. Brewer (William A.), *t*
r John Peacock, *d*
r Lucy C. Wyeth (Mrs. J. W. Bemis),
November. *r* Asher C. Palmer,
r Mrs. Anna M. Palmer (Asher C.),
r Eliza C. Bubier (Mrs. James Gregory), *t*
Mrs. Abigail Watson. *d*

1850.

January. *r* John Tennent, *d*
r Mrs. Elizabeth Tennent (John), *d*
r Jane Tennent (Mrs. Stafford),
James Anderson,
r Jane Ross (Mrs. James Anderson),
July. *r* John Barnes,
r Mrs. Elizabeth J. Barnes (John),
Robert Foster, *d*
Mrs. Isabella Foster (Robert),
Adeline M. Ireson,
September. *r* George W. White, *t*
r Mrs. Eliza White (George W.), *t*
r Catharine Hazlett (Mrs. Wilson),
r Isabella Hazlett,
Henry Z. Hosmer, *t*
Rutharia Bates,
Harriet Torrey (Mrs. L. R. Pearson),
Lucy Torrey,
Julia Ann Russell, *d*
Mary Hayes (Mrs. True Blake), *t*
Louisa R. Green,
Mary Louisa Ropes,
November. Harriet D. Edson (Mrs. Simpson), *t*
Abby S. Thayer,
r Esther C. Sargent, *d*
r Mary S. Sargent,
r Abigail R. Sargent, *d*
r Nancy Sargent, *d*
r Mrs. Mary M. Parker (Joel),
r Thomas Tennent. *t*

1851.

January. *r* Richard Stewart, *t*
r Mrs. Mary Stewart (Richard), *t*
r William Stewart, *t*
r Mrs. Sarah Shedd,
May. *r* Martha P. Carter, *t*
July. Thaddeus W. Harris, *d*
r Eliza Bates,
November. *r* Gardiner G. Hubbard,
r Mrs. Gertrude M. Hubbard (Gardiner G.),
r Joseph W. Hubbard, *t*
r Mrs. Olive S. Hubbard (Joseph W.). *t*

1852.

May. Joseph B. Tufts. *t*

1853.

March. *r* Samuel Walker, *t*
r Mrs. Lilias Walker (Samuel), *t*
r Margaret McAdam, *t*
r Mrs. Eliza J. Brown (Daniel), *d*
r Jeremiah E. Chamberlain, *t*
r Susan Wright (Mrs. John Young),
r Ellis G. Jones, *t*
r Mrs. Dinah E. Jones (Ellis G.), *t*
James Hosmer, *t*
John Emery Horr, *t*
Mary Hosmer, *t*
Susan E. Brewer (Mrs. A. S. Wiley),
Helen A. Palmer (Mrs. Henry Mason), *t*
Anna G. Palmer,
Frances L. E. Hastings (Mrs. Moses Clarke), *d*
Sarah A. Hayes (Mrs. J. Learned),
Emily Hayes,
Mrs. Hannah M. Wood (Charles P.), *t*
" Abigail Alden (Harvey),
May. *r* Mrs. Constance Guyot, *d*
r Arnold H. Guyot, *t*
r Mrs. Constance C. Chollet, *d*
r Ernest Sandoz, *t*
r Mrs. Elizabeth Sandoz, *t*

November. Mrs. Lucy Stickney, *d*
" Helen H. Stickney (Nathaniel S.),
James P. Melledge,
Mrs. Sarah Jane Melledge (James P.),
r Otis Danforth,
r Mrs. Selina Danforth (Otis).

1854.

March. *r* John C. Farnham,
r Mrs. Sarah T. Farnham (John C.),
Mary L. Hayes,
May. *r* George H. Deane,
r Mrs. Maria H. Deane (George H.),
r William C. Kerr, *t*
Mary J. Colburn (Mrs. T. H. Brewer),
July. *r* Charles A. Green,
r Mrs. Catharine M. Green (Charles A.),
James M. Lassell, *d*
November. *r* James R. Morse, *t*
r Mrs. Lorette M. Morse (James R.), *t*
Frances A. Taylor. *d*

1855.

January. *r* Hugh Keys, *t*
r Mrs. Emma C. Kerr (W. C.), *t*
May. *r* " Lydia H. W. Dodge,
Margaret Walker, *t*
July. *r* John Harmon, *t*
r Mrs. Mary A. Harmon (John), *t*
Benjamin Topliff, *t*
September. Mary Elizabeth Walton,
November. Mrs. Susan L. Capelle (Thomas).

1856.

March. *r* Mrs. Sarah Ann Comerford, *t*
Martha J. Hayes (Mrs. J. D. Norris),
May. John Murray, Jr., *t*
Mrs. Julia Topliff (Benjamin), *t*
Julia M. Topliff, *d*
r Margaret Jackson,
July. Mary Ann Comerford, *t*

July. *r* John A. Whipple,
r Mrs. Elizabeth M. Whipple (John A.),
Jane Wright (Mrs. Thomas Irving),
Mary A. Wright,
November. *r* Francis E. Whitcomb, *t*
r Mrs. Lydia Whitcomb (Francis E.), *t*
Maria Topliff. *d*

1857.

March. Charlotte F. Bates,
May. Mrs. Hannah L. Huntington (James),
r Henry H. Prentice,
July. *r* Mrs. Sarah W. Porter, *t*
Sarah M. Farnham (Mrs. Fletcher Bates).

1858.

March. *r* John C. Allen, *t*
r Mrs. Hannah Allen (John C.), *d*
r Mary McCutcheon, *t*
Esther C. Parsons, *d*
July. *r* George L. Ward,
Mrs. Caroline P. Ward (George L.),
John L. Sands,
r Mrs. Sarah A. Sands (John L.), *d*
r " Marvilla Houghton (William), *d*
r Margaret Rainey (Mrs. Joseph Hazlett),
Arthur Merrill, *d*
Mrs. Sarah E Merrill (Arthur),
" Charlotte W. Tucker (Elliott P.),
" Elizabeth Perkins (Levi),
James A. Shedd,
William E. Shedd,
Eunice P. Balch (Mrs. W. E. Shedd),
Fanny F. Shedd, *t*
William T. Gibson,
Milton A. L. Walton, *t*
Charles P. Deane,
Charles A. Stevens,
Abigail L. Prentiss,
Sarah W. Sargent,
Jessie Walker (Mrs. Kincaid),

July. Theresa A. Stevens (Mrs. W. Newton),
Harriet Hayes (Mrs. W. A. Orcutt),
Mary S. Thayer,
Isabel L. Barry, *t*
September. Benjamin F. Sands, *t*
George H. Brewer, *t*
November. Josiah K. Bennett, *t*
Fletcher Bates,
Julia H. Kimball,
r Mary McCutchins.

1859.

January. *r* Charles T. Russell *(Deacon)*,
r Mrs. Sarah E. Russell (Charles T.),
r " Charlotte Sanger (Ralph),
r " Mary G. Brinckerhoff (Isaac), *t*
William Houghton, *t*
March. *r* Mrs. Mary Hadley,
Caroline A. Sands (Mrs. J. I. W. Burgess), *t*
Harriet E. Sands,
William A. Orcutt, *e*
May. *r* Henry Mason,
r Mrs. Helen P. Mason (Henry),
Margaret Hazlett (Mrs. A. Watson), *d*
July. *r* Jonas Wood,
r Mrs. Mary R. Woodbury, *t*
September. Elizabeth B. Russell, *t*
Josephine E. Russell, *t*
November. *r* Mary E. Snow (Mrs. Leonard),
r Solomon H. Brackett. *t*

1860.

March. *r* Dorcas H. Langmaid (Mrs. Samuel H.),
r Mrs. Abby R. Gillett,
May. *r* Elbridge G. Alden, *d*
r Mrs. Sophia D. Alden (Elbridge G.),
r John C. Heymer,
r Mrs. Caroline M. Heymer (John C.),
r Elizabeth Stewart,
July. *r* Zenas W. Bliss, *t*
November. *r* Locke Etheridge.

1861.

January.	Henry Barry, *t*
	Mrs. Edith M. Barry (Henry), *t*
	Daniel Brown,
	Mrs. Eliza Ann Brown (Daniel),
	r Sarah Hazlett (Mrs. Thomas Gibson),
May.	Celestia F. Barnes (Mrs. Francis Flint),
July.	Mary Louisa Bullard,
September.	Miriam B. Homer,
	r Ivory Sands,
	r Mrs. Eliza D. Sands (Ivory).

1862.

January.	Charles G. Green,
March.	Mary Augusta Bates,
	Esther A. Bates,
May.	Susan Robinson (Mrs. Thomas Watson), *t*
	Anna E. Albro, *t*
July.	*r* James D. Norris,
	r Anna Beatty (Mrs. J. Hackett),
	Mary E. Homer,
	r Julius Taylor,
	r Mrs. Sarah E. Taylor (Julius),
	r Mary A. Morrill,
	r Mrs. Margaret L. Kerr (John C.),
	Anna L. Pratt (Mrs. George H. Smith),
	Alice E. Taylor,
	Mary F. M. Taylor,
	Mary E. Evans,
November.	*r* John H. Partridge,
	r Mrs. Susannah P. Partridge (John H.).

1863.

January.	Mary Ann Waddell (Mrs. John Hayes),
March.	Mrs. Margaret Jane Lovell.

1864.

March.	*r* Mrs. Abigail Avery,
	r " Louisa A. Sawin (Nathaniel D.),
	r Helen Marr,
May.	*r* Mary E. Paine, *t*

May. *r* Ellen A. Paine,
r Flavius J. Cook,
r George C. S. Southwick,
July. Mrs. Phœbe B. Rust,
r Anne C. Rust,
r John Templeton,
r Mrs. Eliza Templeton (John), *d*
Sarah Whipple.

1865.

January. Mrs. Martha J. Evans (William),
March. *r* Mrs. Sarah Gates,
r Daniel D. Fuller,
May. *r* George B. Roberts, *t*
r Mary Ann Johnston (Mrs. Farmer). *d*

1866.

January. *r* Legh R. Pearson,
March. *r* Mrs. Emily B. Shedd (James A.),
July. *r* Francis Flint,
r Mrs. Harriet N. Parker (Horatio G.), *d*
George H. Beaman,
Allen H. Fletcher,
Francis W. Dolloff,
Charles F. Stratton,
William J. Stewart,
J. Gardner Osgood,
John Young,
Richard Dolton, *d*
Mrs. Mary A. Dolton (Richard),
Elizabeth C. Bullard,
Catherine P. Green,
Alice R. Green,
Esther J. Alden,
Emma G. Alden,
Rowena R. Clarke (Mrs. C. E. Coombs),
Anna R. Bates,
Sarah E. D. Shedd, *t*
Martha P. Snow,
Mary Amanda Russell, *t*
Caroline Adelaide Merrill,

July. Addie E. Walton,
Anna A. Whipple,
Ella M. Whipple,
September. *r* John Fullerton,
Mary A. Ritchie,
November. Mrs. Martha C. Kinsley (W.), *t*
Andrew Stewart.

1867.

January. Charles T. Russell, Jr.

Rev. Alexander McKenzie, Pastor. January 24, 1867.

March. *r* Ephraim P. Whitman,
r Mrs. Sophronia A. Whitman (Ephraim P.),
r Charles P. Wood,
r Mrs. Hannah M. Wood (Charles P.),
r " Hannah Somerby,
r " Priscilla N. Pomeroy,
r Rachel A. Pomeroy,
r Emma F. Pomeroy (Mrs. W. H. D. Eaton),
r Mrs. Clara C. Osgood,
r Abbie A. Osgood,
r Mrs. Sarah G. Osgood (George),
r Adeline H. Rogers,
r Mrs. Lucy W. Keyes,
Emma F. Hayes,
Susan E. Thayer,
Elizabeth A. Hutchinson,
Sarah J. Stewart,
Mary F. Whipple,
May. *r* Mrs. Hannah Boyd (William),
r Elizabeth J. Ward,
Mary Leila Horsford,
Mary Katherine Horsford,
Gertrude H. Horsford,
November. *r* Mrs. Caroline M. Howe (Thomas J.),
r Irene F. Sanger.

1868.

January. *r* William Sinclair, *t*
r Mrs. Elizabeth Sinclair (William),

January. Sarah L. Russell,
Mary L. Gale,
March. *r* Samuel H. Scudder,
r Mrs. Jeannie B. Scudder (Samuel H.),
r Mary E. Blatchford,
r Caroline H. Blatchford,
r Samuel F. Rugg,
r Mrs. Mary Rugg (Samuel F.),
r Mrs. Mary B. Gregg,
r James B. Gregg,
r Mrs. Sarah A. Fox (Henry H.),
r Charles E. Fox,
r Mrs. Emma L. Fuller (Arthur B.),
r Edward F. Buckminster,
r Mrs. Jennie B. Nesbitt, *t*
r " Christiana Nesbitt,
r Alice Nesbitt,
May. *r* Josiah Merrill,
r Mrs. Henrietta C. Merrill (Josiah), *d*
r " Harriette Pierce (Charles R.),
r " Eliza E. Bates (James V.),
r Isabella McCoy,
r Eliza M. Judkins,
r Mary McCarrigle, *t*
Gustave Weinschenk,
Mrs. Eunice W. Weinschenk (Gustave),
James H. Cate,
Mrs. Mary L. Cate (James H.),
" Susan O. Sawin (Moses M.),
" Ellen M. Priest (Edward E.), *d*
Annie N. Ward,
Nellie S. Johnson,
Sarah E. Sands,
Harriet E. Sands,
Elizabeth A. Gould,
Helen R. Bartholomew (Mrs. W. D. Hammond), *t*
Delia R. Chadbourne (Mrs. C. F. Stratton),
Adelia Dunham,
Julia Dunham,
Grace E. Stevens,
Emily C. Osgood,

May. George H. Johnson,
Henry B. Wenzell,
Henry F. Merrill,
Martin W. Sands,
July. Mrs. Sophia W. Dolloff (William J.),
Sarah F. Hall,
Ellen S. Dwight,
September. Andrew B. McGahy,
Mrs. Jane S. McGahy (Andrew B.),
Abbie M. Hall (Mrs. S. P. Sharples),
November. *r* James M. W. Hall,
r Mrs. Orianna A. Hall (James M. W.),
r Zenas W. Bliss,
r Mrs. Sophia M. Bliss (Zenas W.).

1869.

January. *r* Charles H. Whitney,
r Mrs. Abby A. Whitney (Charles H.) *d*,
r Annie E. Whitney,
r Mary A. Whitney,
r Hattie E. Whitney,
r Mrs. Mary T. Wyeth (Jonas),
r Henry F. Johnson,
r Mrs. Eunice S. Johnson (Henry F.),
r Charles W. Munroe,
r Mrs. Susan M. Munroe (Charles W.),
Susan M. Munroe,
r Mrs. Ellen L. Packard (Frederick),
" Mary D. Lyon (Leonard),
Charlotte E. Peirce,
Henrietta Anderson,
March. *r* Robert F. Pennell,
r John F. Dwight,
r Mrs. Sally A. Dwight (John F.),
r Susan P. Colburn,
r Helen E. Morey,
May. *r* Charles C. Beaman,
r Mrs. Mary A. Beaman (Charles C.),
r Laureston L. Stone,
r Mrs. Margaret J. Stone (Laureston L.),
r " Isabella Milliken (James S.).

May. *r* Mrs. Charlotte E. Sprague (William F.),
r Eunice W. Field,
r Ellen M. Rugg (Mrs. H. M. Marshall),
Mrs. Almira E. Tilden (Eustis),
Minnie A. Johnson,
July. Annie B. Stephens,
Sarah E. Langley,
Grace Fuller,
r Mrs. Elizabeth Frost (Edmund),
September. *r* Elinor M. Howells (William D.),
November. *r* Mary H. True,
r Frank H. Foster,
Edward A. Presbrey,
Mrs. Ruth W. Presbrey (Edward A.).

1870.

January. *r* William F. Stark,
r Mrs. Sarah L. Stark (William F.),
r " Lavinia H. Weeks,
r " Emily A Burleigh (John A.),
r " Margaret S. Gordon (John),
r Barbara McKay,
r Maggie A. Fickett,
Mary Gardiner Horsford,
March. *r* Aaron H. Safford,
r Mrs. Sarah Safford (Aaron H.),
May. " Mary J. Thurston (George A.),
Christina Kelley,
Mary Gillis,
Sarah McKinnon (Mrs. L. McDonald), *t*
Margaret C. Waugh,
Katie McEachan,
July. *r* Mrs. Elizabeth Y. Hayes (Henry Y.),
September. *r* Louisa S. Munroe,
November. *r* John L. Hildreth.
Mrs. Achsah B. C. Hildreth (John L.),
r Mrs. Amelia F. Alden (James B.),
r Margaret Mellon,
r Josiah G. Willis,
James C. Merrill.

1871.

January.	*r* John S. Parker,
March.	Effie Kelley,
	Katie J. Rogers,
	Bessie D. Ferguson,
	Ann Richards,
	Florence V. Stickney,
	Lizzie J. Brown,
	Mary Gertrude Parker,
May.	Mrs. Ellen A. Whitman (Francis H.),
	r Mary L. Sackett.

PRESENT MEMBERS.

MALES.

Albro, John S.
Anderson, James

Barnes, John
Bates, Fletcher
Beaman, Charles C.
Beaman, George H.
Bliss, Zenas W.
Brown Daniel
Buckminster, Edward F.

Cate, James H.
Chandler, Josiah
Clark, Benjamin A.
Cook, Flavius J.

Danforth, Otis
Deane, Charles P.
Deane, George H.
Dolloff, Francis W.
Dwight, John F.

Etheridge, Locke

Farnham, John C.
Farwell, Stephen T.
Fletcher, Allen H.
Flint, Francis
Foster, Frank H.
Fox, Charles E.
Fuller, Daniel D.
Fullerton, John

Gray, Asa
Green, Charles A.
Green, Charles G.
Greenough, William
Gregg, James B.
Gibson, William T.
Giles, Joel

Hall, James M. W.
Hayes, Edmund
Hayes, Luther S.
Heymer, John C.
Hildreth, John L.
Homer, Charles S.
Homer, Charles W.
Horsford, Eben N.
Hubbard, Gardiner G.

Johnson, George H.
Johnson, Henry F.

Keys, Hugh

Lerned, Thomas P.

Mason, Henry
McGahy, Andrew B.
Melledge, James P.
Merrill, Henry F.
Merrill, James C.
Merrill, Josiah

Mumler, Frederick A.
Munroe, Charles W.

Norris, James D.

Osgood, J. Gardner

Palmer, Asher C.
Parker, John S.
Partridge, John H.
Pearson, Legh R.
Pennell, Robert F.
Pickett, Samuel
Prentice, Henry H.
Presbrey, Edward A.

Rugg, Samuel F.
Russell, Charles T.
Russell, Charles T., Jr.

Safford, Aaron H.
Sands, Ivory
Sands, John L.
Sands, Martin W.
Saunders, George S.
Saunders, William A.
Scudder, Samuel H.
Shedd, James A.
Shedd, William E.
Stark, William F.
Stevens, Charles A.
Southwick, George C. S.
Stone, Laureston L.
Stratton, Charles
Stratton, Charles F.
Stewart, Andrew
Stewart, William J.

Taylor, Julius
Templeton, John
Thurston, Lyman

Ward, George L.
Weinschenk, Gustave
Wenzell, Henry B.
Whipple, John
Whipple, John A.
Whitman, Ephraim P.
Whitney, Charles H.
Whittemore, Amos
Wood, Charles P.
Wood, Jonas
Willis, Josiah G.

Young, John

FEMALES.

Alden, Mrs. Abigail
Alden, Mrs. Amelia F.
Alden, Emma G.
Alden, Esther J.
Alden, Mrs. Sophia D.
Anderson, Henrietta
Anderson, Mrs. Jane R.
Avery, Mrs. Abigail

Barnes, Mrs. Elizabeth J.
Bates, Anna R.
Bates, Charlotte F.
Bates, Eliza
Bates, Mrs. Eliza E.
Bates, Esther A.
Bates, Mary Augusta
Bates, Rutharia
Bates, Mrs. Sarah M.
Bates, Mrs. Susan
Beaman, Mrs. Mary A.
Bemis, Mrs. Lucy C.
Blatchford, Caroline H.

Blatchford, Mary E.
Bliss, Mrs. Sophia M.
Bowman, Harriet C.
Boyd, Mrs. Hannah
Brown, Mrs. Eliza Ann
Brown, Lizzie J.
Brown, Lucy
Brewer, Mrs. Mary J.
Bullard, Elizabeth C.
Bullard, Mary Louisa
Burleigh, Mrs. Emily A.

Capelle, Mrs. Susan L.
Cate, Mrs. Mary L.
Clark, Mrs. Almira
Colburn, Susan P.
Conant, Mrs. Ruth
Coombs, Mrs. Rowena R.

Dana, Elizabeth E.
Danforth, Mrs. Selina
Deane, Mrs. Maria H.
Delano, Lorana P.
Dodge, Mrs. Lydia H. W.
Dolloff, Mrs. Sophia W.
Dolton, Mrs. Mary A.
Dunham, Adelia
Dunham, Julia
Dunham, Mrs. Lovey
Dwight, Ellen S.
Dwight, Mrs. Sally A.

Eaton, Mrs. Emma F.
Evans, Mrs. Martha J.
Evans, Mary E.

Farnham, Mrs. Sarah T.
Farwell, Mrs. Elizabeth C.
Ferguson, Bessie D.
Fickett, Maggie A.
Field, Eunice W.
Flint, Mrs. Celestia F.
Follett, Mrs. Eunice G.
Foster, Mrs. Isabella
Fox, Mrs. Sarah A.
Frost, Mrs. Elizabeth
Fuller, Mrs. Eliza J.
Fuller, Mrs. Emma L.
Fuller, Grace

Gale, Mary L.
Gardiner, Mrs. Mary J.
Gates, Mrs. Sarah
Gibson, Mrs. Sarah H.
Gillett, Mrs. Abby R.
Gillis, Mary
Gordon, Mrs. Margaret S.
Gould, Elizabeth A.
Gould, Mary S.
Green, Alice R.
Green, Mrs. Catharine M.
Green, Catherine P.
Green, Louisa R.
Greenough, Mrs. Sarah
Gregg, Mrs. Mary B.
Griffin, Mrs. Caroline
Griffin, Mrs. Hannah H.

Hackett, Mrs. Anna B.
Hadley, Mrs. Mary
Hall, Mrs. Orianna A.
Hall, Sarah F.
Hall, Mrs. Sarah S.
Hartness, Mrs. Margaret G.
Hayes, Mrs. Eliza
Hayes, Mrs. Elizabeth Y.
Hayes, Mrs. Emeline S.
Hayes, Emily
Hayes, Emma F.
Hayes, Mrs. Mary Ann

Hayes, Mary L.
Hayes, Mrs. Miriam G.
Hazlett, Isabella
Hazlett, Mrs. Margaret R.
Heymer, Mrs. Caroline M.
Hildreth, Mrs. Achsah B. C.
Homer, Mrs. Adeline D.
Homer, Mrs. Henrietta M.
Homer, Mary E.
Homer, Miriam B.
Horsford, Gertrude H.
Horsford, Mary Gardiner
Horsford, Mary Katherine
Horsford, Mary Leila
Howe, Mrs. Caroline M.
Howells, Elinor M.
Hubbard, Mrs. Gertrude M.
Huntington, Mrs. Hannah L.
Hutchinson, Elizabeth A.

Ireson, Adeline M.
Irving, Mrs. Jane

Jackson, Margaret
Johnson, Mrs. Eunice S.
Johnson, Minnie A.
Johnson, Nellie S.
Judkins, Eliza M.

Kelley, Christina
Kelley, Effie
Kennard, Mrs. Lydia A.
Kerr, Mrs. Margaret L.
Keyes, Mrs. Lucy W.
Kimball, Julia H.
Kincaid, Mrs. Jessie W.

Langley, Sarah E.
Langmaid, Mrs. Dorcas H.
Learned, Mrs. Sarah A.
Lovell, Mrs. Margaret Jane
Lyman, Charlotte A.
Lyman, Mary
Lyon, Mrs. Mary D.

Marr, Helen
Marshall, Mrs. Ellen M.
Mason, Mrs. Helen P.
McCoy, Isabella
McCutchins, Mary
McEachan, Katie
McGahy, Mrs. Jane B.
McKay, Barbara
Melledge, Mrs. Sarah Jane
Mellon, Margaret
Merrill, Caroline Adelaide
Merrill, Mrs. Mary
Merrill, Mrs. Sarah E.
Milliken, Mrs. Isabella
Morey, Helen E.
Morrill, Mary A.
Munroe, Louisa S.
Munroe, Sarah
Munroe, Mrs. Susan
Munroe, Mrs. Susan M.
Munroe, Susan M.

Nesbitt, Alice
Nesbitt, Mrs. Christiana
Newton, Mrs. Theresa A.
Norris, Mrs. Martha J.

Orcutt, Mrs. Harriet H.
Osgood, Abbie A.
Osgood, Mrs. Clara C.
Osgood, Emily C.
Osgood, Mrs. Sarah G.

Packard, Mrs. Ellen L.
Paine, Ellen A.

Palmer, Anna G.
Palmer, Mrs. Anna M.
Parker, Eliza C.
Parker, Lydia
Parker, Mary Gertrude
Parker, Mrs. Mary M.
Parker, Susan
Partridge, Mrs. Susannah P.
Peacock, Mrs. Margaret
Pearson, Mrs. Harriet T.
Peirce, Charlotte E.
Perkins, Mrs. Elizabeth
Pickett, Mary E.
Pickett, Mrs. Nancy
Pierce, Mrs. Harriette
Pomeroy, Mrs. Priscilla N.
Pomeroy, Rachel A.
Prentiss, Abigail L.
Presbrey, Mrs. Ruth W.

Ramsay, Catharine
Richards, Ann
Ritchie, Mary A.
Rogers, Adeline H.
Rogers, Katie J.
Ropes, Mary Louisa
Ropes, Sarah
Rugg, Mrs. Mary
Russell, Mrs. Cynthia
Russell, Mrs. Sarah E.
Russell, Sarah L.
Rust, Anne C.
Rust, Mrs. Phœbe B.

Sackett, Mary L.
Safford, Mrs. Sarah
Sands, Mrs. Eliza D.
Sands, Harriet E.
Sands, Harriet E.
Sands, Sarah E.
Sanger, Mrs. Charlotte
Sanger, Irene F.
Sargent, Mary S.
Sargent, Sarah W.
Saunders, Mrs. Lucy C.
Saunders, Mrs. Mary P.
Saunders, Mrs. Sarah
Sawin, Mrs. Louisa A.
Sawin Mrs. Susan O.
Sawyer, Lucy D.
Scudder, Mrs. Jeannie B.
Sharples, Mrs. Abbie M.
Shedd, Mrs. Emily B.
Shedd, Mrs. Eunice P.
Shedd, Mrs. Sarah
Sinclair, Mrs. Elizabeth
Smith, Mrs. Anna L.
Snow, Martha P.
Snow, Mrs. Mary E.
Somerby, Mrs. Hannah
Soule, Clarissa
Sprague, Mrs. Charlotte E.
Stafford, Mrs. Jane T.
Stark, Mrs. Sarah L.
Stephens, Annie B.
Stevens, Mrs. Anne G.
Stevens, Grace E.
Stewart, Elizabeth
Stewart, Mrs. Ellen
Stewart, Sarah J.
Stone, Mrs. Margaret J.
Stickney, Florence V.
Stickney, Mrs. Helen H.
Stratton, Mrs. Delia R.
Stratton, Mrs. Eunice

Taylor, Alice E.
Taylor, Mary F. M.
Taylor, Mrs. Sarah E.
Thayer, Abby S.

Thayer, Mrs. Mary
Thayer, Mary S.
Thayer, Susan E.
Thurston, Delia A.
Thurston, Mrs. Louisa S.
Thurston, Mrs. Mary J.
Tilden, Mrs. Almira E.
Torrey, Lucy
True, Mary H.
Tucker, Mrs. Charlotte W.

Walton, Addie E.
Walton, Mary Elizabeth
Walton, Mrs. Harriet
Ward, Annie N.
Ward, Mrs. Caroline P.
Ward, Elizabeth J.
Watson, Mrs. Susan R.
Waugh, Margaret C.
Weeks, Mrs. Lavinia H.
Weinschenk, Mrs. Eunice W.
Wells, Eliza Ann
Whipple, Anna A.
Whipple, Mrs. Elizabeth M.
Whipple, Ella M.
Whipple, Mrs. John
Whipple, Mary F.
Whipple, Sarah
White, Mrs. Sarah J.
Whitman, Mrs. Ellen A.
Whitman, Mrs. Sophronia A.
Whitney, Annie E.
Whitney, Hattie E.
Whitney, Mary A.
Whittemore, Mrs. Almira
Wiley, Mrs. Susan E.
Willard Elizabeth L.
Willard, Mrs. Lucy
Wilson, Mrs. Catharine H.
Wood, Mrs. Hannah M.
Wright, Mary A.
Wyeth, Mrs. Mary T.
Wyeth, Mrs. Zoa D.

Young, Mrs. Susan W.

CPSIA information can be obtained
at www.ICGtesting.com
Printed in the USA
LVHW041234170323
741847LV00006B/558

9 783382 128685